Barbara Taylor Bradford has written twenty-? novels. Her debut novel, *A Woman of Substance*, was an international bestseller. Barbara's books have sold more than eighty-five million copies in over ninety countries and forty languages. Ten mini-series and television films have been made of her books. In 2007, Barbara was awarded an OBE by the Queen for her services to literature.

Also by Barbara Taylor Bradford

Series
THE EMMA HARTE SAGA
A Woman of Substance
Hold the Dream
To Be the Best
Emma's Secret
Unexpected Blessings
Just Rewards
Breaking the Rules

THE RAVENSCAR TRILOGY
The Ravenscar Dynasty
Heirs of Ravenscar
Being Elizabeth

Others
Voice of the Heart
Act of Will
The Women in His Life
Remember
Angel
Everything to Gain
Dangerous to Know
Love in Another Town
Her Own Rules
A Secret Affair
Power of a Woman
A Sudden Change of Heart
Where You Belong
The Triumph of Katie Byrne
Three Weeks in Paris
Playing the Game
Letter from a Stranger
Secrets from the Past
Cavendon Hall

Hidden

Barbara Taylor Bradford

HARPER

Harper
An imprint of HarperCollins*Publishers*
77–85 Fulham Palace Road,
Hammersmith, London W6 8JB

www.harpercollins.co.uk

First published in Great Britain by
HarperCollins*Publishers* 2014

A catalogue record for this book is
available from the British Library

ISBN: 978-0-00-755019-7

Set in ITC Stone Serif 12/16pt by
Palimpsest Book Production Limited, Falkirk, Stirlingshire

Printed and bound in Great Britain by
Clays Ltd, St Ives plc

Hidden

One

Claire dressed in a hurry. If she was late there would be questions, and she couldn't risk that today.

She pulled on black leggings, a black cashmere turtleneck jumper and tall, butter-soft boots. She had the sort of body that was easy to dress: tall, lean, flexible. She looped a scarf around her neck and secured it with a vintage brooch. A chunky bracelet, gold earrings and a basic black uniform was turned into something special and uniquely hers.

It was a gift, she knew, this different way of seeing fashion; one that had propelled her from sales assistant to head of the famous personal shopping department at Gilda, the most exclusive store in New York. It was said that she dressed everyone from the First Lady to Lady Gaga, but Claire would never confirm that.

She was a woman who knew how to keep secrets.

Claire examined her reflection in the mirror. Her skin was still flawless at forty-two. The wide-set sea-blue eyes were steady as she studied herself. She knew, from hard experience, that the reddish tint spreading over half her face would soon turn a bluish purple, then green, and finally a sickly yellowish brown.

With grim determination, and a skilled hand, Claire set to work trying to cover the still tender bruises. A mixture of yellow and white cover-up first, the green, colour-correcting primer, then a coating of foundation, thick but subtle. She rarely wore makeup of any sort, and if the coverage was too obvious, a friend would notice. She added a bit of carefully placed blusher, and a bright lipstick to focus the attention. As an afterthought, she pulled out a pair of oversized sunglasses with pink lenses from the drawer, and put them on. People wore sunglasses inside all the time.

You don't, she reminded herself, and reluctantly removed the glasses, shook her mane of rich auburn hair loose from its clip and inspected her handiwork.

A sob caught in her throat. This time her skill had failed her. The carefully covered bruises looked like what they were – battle scars. She hit speed-dial on her mobile.

'It's just a slight fever,' she told Sasha, praying that her friend wouldn't sense that she was lying. 'I'm going to crawl into bed and watch reruns of *Downton Abbey*.'

'Sounds decadent! Maybe I'll stop by after lunch and join you?'

'No!' Claire did her best to sound light-hearted. 'I'm a germ factory. Toxic.'

'If you recall, I have the immune system of a dinosaur!' Sasha laughed. 'I haven't been sick since your daughter shared her chicken pox with me fourteen years ago.'

Claire couldn't help smiling. Sasha always had that effect on her, even in the worst of times. They had been best friends since meeting on the train in 1992. Twenty years ago. Then they had been young brides filled with hope and excitement, and dreams of happily ever after.

Soon there were four of them who met every weekday on the 8:27 Westport to Grand Central express train. Julia and Paulina got on the train in Fairfield, and saved the four-seater in the third carriage back. Claire and Sasha got on in Westport, with coffee and croissants. On that train to Manhattan the four of them had shared their lives: the triumphs as well as the struggles to balance the careers they loved with family life. More recently, they admitted their mixed feelings now that the children they practically raised together had left for college. Most discussed their marital troubles.

Not Claire.

Her husband, Mark, had long held important positions in the US government. Currently he was special advisor to the President on Middle Eastern affairs. Even a whiff of scandal would wreck everything he had spent his life working towards.

At least that's what he was always telling Claire.

So she kept her problems to herself, except where Sasha was concerned. You just couldn't lie to Sasha. The other women, too, sensed something was amiss in the seemingly perfect marriage of Claire and Mark Saunders. They said nothing out of love for their friend, but they worried.

'May I remind you, Sasha, that the dinosaurs are extinct? Go to lunch. Tell Julia and Paulie I'll be there next Saturday without fail.' She tried to keep her voice light. 'Same time, same place.'

Claire finished the call quickly. She drifted into the long gallery that ran the length of the house, and put a match to one of the fires that Mr Atkins, the caretaker, kept laid in each of the home's five fireplaces.

It was a large room; the house had been designed by a famous architect and all the rooms were airy and spacious and flooded with light. Claire had decorated the graceful space so that there were cosy corners for one or two, as well as ample space for the grand receptions that were part of Mark's job.

She curled up next to the crackling fire and studied the vases of roses that seemed to occupy every surface in the large room. So many roses. Too many roses, as always yellow and pink. The doorbell began to ring over and over, pulling her out of her dark thoughts. More roses, she thought, heading for the hall. She was limping a bit now from the falls she had taken last night. She pulled the door open, but instead of the delivery man from Petals there stood Sasha.

Sasha was as petite and blonde as Claire was tall and exotic. She was one of the few female producers working on television commercials. In that world many men had mistaken her Barbie-Doll prettiness for softness or, worse, lack of intelligence. Few made that mistake twice.

'Chicken soup from Gold's Deli,' Sasha announced, waving a shopping bag as she marched inside. 'Better than Lemsip!'

Claire stood frozen in the doorway.

'Where are we with *Downton*?' Sasha's words

trailed off as she entered the gallery and saw the flowers: vase after vase after vase.

Claire still hadn't moved.

'Dear God.' The words came out in a whisper. 'So many.'

Sasha turned back to her friend, fearing what she would see but knowing. 'It must have been bad this time.' Sasha tenderly examined her friend's damaged face. 'Very bad. Oh, Claire.'

'I told you not to come.' Claire fought back tears. She hurried past Sasha and into the gallery, trying to escape the worry she saw on her friend's face.

'Work again? He still wants you to give up your job, your career?' Sasha didn't wait for an answer.

'He worries about me commuting,' Claire murmured.

Sasha was following her. 'Are you limping? Claire, you're limping!'

'It's nothing. It was a small thing.'

'A *small thing*? You look like you've been through World War Three! What is *wrong* with him?'

Claire started to defend him, but stopped herself. She knew she was lying to Sasha – and to herself. 'You can't tell anyone. *Please* . . .'

'Shhhhh.' The words were muffled as Sasha

sat on the arm of the chair and put her arms around her friend, stroking her hair with tenderness. 'It's okay. It's going to be okay.'

They were both weeping now.

'We have to find a way to stop him, Claire. We *must*. It's getting worse. Each time, it's worse.'

'It's just this Middle East thing he's working on for the President! Things are out of control over there—'

Sasha cut her off, fighting to hide her frustration. 'It's not the Middle East, Claire! It's him! Mark is the one who is out of control. And if we don't find a way to stop him, one of these days he's going to kill you!'

Two

Dusk had its own strange colour in Connecticut during those first days of spring. After the grey winter, a pink haze began to steal over the gardens, promising better things ahead.

The two women sat side by side, trays on laps, watching the light show through the windows of the conservatory, which Claire had turned into a study. A vase, stuffed with two dozen pink and yellow roses, sat on the table that held a flat-screen television.

Claire used the remote to switch off the set. 'Now that was really good,' she sighed.

'Which?' Sasha asked. 'Gold's chicken soup or Lady Edith from *Downton Abbey* getting what was coming to her for gossiping about her sister?'

'Both.' Claire reached for her friend's hand. 'Thank you for staying with me.'

'If you'd allow it, I'd stand guard over you with a shotgun until Mark leaves for Cairo.'

Claire looked out of the windows at the fading sunlight, desperate to change the subject.

'Today is Deborah's birthday. Twenty-one. Can you believe it?'

'How could I forget? I'm her godmother.' Sasha knew Claire so well, knew she needed a moment now, some space to think, so she didn't press. But she was far from finished with the problem. 'Have you spoken with our little musical genius yet?' she asked.

'She had classes all day, and then she and a friend have tickets to some big concert at the Albert Hall. I'll call soon.'

'What time is it in London?'

'Four hours ahead. So I have time.'

'Ah . . .' Sasha moved so she could look at Claire. 'I was just wondering. How would *you* handle it, if I told you someone was hurting Deborah?'

'What are you talking about?' Claire exclaimed.

Sasha fixed her with her laser-like gaze. 'I don't mean for real. What if someone was hurting her like Mark hurts you? What would you do?'

'Don't do this, Sasha. I don't want to talk about it right now. Okay?' Claire started to get out of the chair. 'I just can't.'

'Don't run away. We have to make a plan. Seriously Claire, we can't do what we've been doing. We have to talk about this.'

'Talk about what?' The man's voice was coming from the doorway. Neither woman moved.

Mark Saunders didn't so much walk as glide into a room, bringing with him a heady mixture of good looks, charm and a certain danger that made him impossible to ignore. At forty-four, he still had the boyish blond looks that women love.

'Hello, darling.' He leaned down to kiss Claire, who was trying desperately to control her trembling.

'Good grief, you look as if someone shot your dog. What's going on?' There was a smile on his face, but he was on full alert, taking the measure of the mood in the room. That was what he did for a living.

He turned his smile on Sasha. 'You look beautiful, as always. How's Jeff? How are the television ads? Still busy persuading the public to buy things they don't need?'

Sasha held his blue eyes but did not return the smile. 'I do what I can.' She sipped her wine, not taking her gaze off Mark. 'And Jeff is fine. I'll tell him you were asking about him.'

Shooting her friend a pleading look, Claire was on her feet. 'I thought you weren't coming home till much later. I would have had dinner—'

'Stop,' he purred, putting an arm around her,

the model of a devoted husband. 'You'll make Sasha think I keep you chained to the stove. So, Sasha, what is it you and Claire *must* talk about? I'm afraid I interrupted you two.'

'Actually, you did,' Sasha now returned his mega-smile with one of her own, equally charming and equally false. 'I'm trying to persuade Claire to have this year's Near and Far charity fund-raiser at Gilda, but the poor lamb is stuck in the past. She's afraid people won't want to drive home from the city late at night.'

Sasha put her wine glass down, and took Claire's as well, so Mark would not notice that her friend's hand was trembling. 'Mark, convince your wife that just because we live in Connecticut, we don't need a passport to cross the border into New York City.'

'I wouldn't try to convince Claire of anything.' The tension in his jaw began to fade. 'She's a woman who knows her own mind.'

'Oh Mark, I know now why you're the star of Washington. Always the diplomat! Claire's a lucky girl.' She kissed her friend on the cheek gingerly so as not to hurt the bruises. 'And, for Heaven's sake, watch where you're walking from now on. Mark, tell her! She walked into the door of the closet this morning, and look what it did to her face.' Sasha made sure that

Mark looked at each and every mark on Claire's beautiful face.

'My dear, how did that happen?' he asked, sounding puzzled.

'You know Claire. She has her head in the clouds and doesn't see the danger around her,' Sasha replied, keeping her voice even.

'You know I'm clumsy.' Claire managed to make her voice sound normal. She didn't dare show Sasha how grateful she was for this little performance.

Mark put one of his perfectly manicured fingers on her cheek and traced the line of bruises. 'This looks wicked. Poor girl. Sasha is right. You must take better care of yourself.'

'I'll be careful, I promise.'

Sasha looked Claire in the eye. 'I'm going to hold you to that promise.'

'So will I,' Mark said, kissing the bruises ever so gently. 'Not to worry, Sasha, I will take care of your friend.'

Sasha had to hurry from the room, because she was very close to punching Mark in the face, just as he had done to Claire.

Three

Claire knew Mark was watching: checking her mood, searching her eyes for secrets, judging each sentence that passed her lips.

He had taken his time with the dinner she had hurriedly prepared after Sasha left. 'Are you sure you won't have another glass of wine? It's really excellent.'

'I don't think so, Mark.'

But he was already pouring. She dutifully thanked him and took a tiny sip. 'What time do you leave for Egypt tomorrow?'

'Early. You know, if you weren't married to that job of yours, you could come with me. See the world.'

Claire managed a small laugh. 'See the inside of a hotel room, you mean. You work night and day on these trips.'

'And what do you do when I'm away?'

Claire knew she needed to be careful. She was silent.

'Do you think you spend too much time with that gang of yours?' he asked.

'Mark, they are my friends; that's all.'

'You see them every day on the train. You'd think that would be enough. But then Saturday too. The unmissable Saturday lunches. What on earth do you find to talk about?'

'You know. The kids, work.'

'Do you tell them about me? What a monster I am?'

'Of course I don't.'

'The roses look nice. Do you like them?'

It was all Claire could do to keep from screaming. 'Very much,' she answered quietly, holding herself still.

'I'm sorry about last night. I feel terrible. But it's almost as if you *enjoy* pushing my buttons.' He stared at her intently.

Claire remained stock still, looking back at him, trying to keep her face blank. 'If you had any idea how much pressure I'm under, how important my work is to the country, maybe you wouldn't push me. Do you think I like hurting you?'

'No. I don't think that.' Carefully, very carefully Claire pushed her chair back, keeping her tone light. 'Are you about finished with dinner? It's late in London, and I want to reach Deborah before she goes to bed.'

'You know college kids. It's her birthday.

She'll be up all night drinking shots with her friends.'

'Mark, she won't. She has to play for the college tomorrow, and she'll want to be in top form. It's the Royal Academy of Music, for heaven's sake.'

'Plenty of musicians party. Can't she have a little fun?' He turned his boyish grin on Claire. 'You're only twenty-one once.'

'You're right, of course.' Her smile was cautious. His love for Deborah always touched her and maybe he really was just being sweet tonight. She needed to stop expecting another explosion. She so wanted to believe it wouldn't happen again. 'I suppose just because our daughter is studying to be a concert pianist doesn't mean she can't be a good-looking party animal like her father.'

'Was he?' Mark was staring into his wine, swirling it around and around, staring into the glass.

'Oh, you still are quite the party boy.' She took another sip. The wine was calming her. 'Good looking, too.' She touched his hand.

'I was talking about her real father.'

He smiled at her again, but this time a chill began climbing her spine. She carefully removed her hand from his, knowing she must tread carefully now, and not contradict him. Mark was at his most dangerous when he was being charming. 'You are the only father she has ever known,' Claire finally said.

'You didn't answer my question,' he shot back, his voice suddenly hard.

Claire got up and started clearing the table.

Mark continued to study his wine. 'I know nothing about your great love. Was he tall? Skinny? Fat? Did he like music? Is that where Deborah's talent comes from?'

Claire took the dishes into the kitchen without a word, trying to push back her emotions.

Mark followed her.

'All I know about Deborah's long-gone daddy is that he walked out on you before she was born. And never looked back. So I don't understand why his memory is so sacred that you refuse to speak of him, won't even tell me his name. Or maybe it's because he's not really gone.'

'When you asked me to marry you, over twenty years ago, when you asked if you could adopt Deborah and raise her as your own, we made an agreement!' Claire's turquoise eyes were blazing now, her fear of him forgotten for a moment. '*I* would never tell Deborah you were not her birth father, and *you* would never ask me about the man who was. I have kept my end of the bargain! All these years, not a word to her, not a hint! You, on the other hand, have been at me constantly in the past few years! What did he look like? Why did he disappear? Does he know he has a daughter?'

'Does he? Do you talk to him sometimes, tell him about her? About me? Is that why you love your job so much? So you can travel all over to be with him?'

'Stop it, Mark.'

He grabbed her wrist roughly, and instinctively she let out a cry of pain. She was already bruised from last night. 'Do you two laugh about how afraid I am that one day Deborah will find him, and won't want anything to do with me?' he hissed in her face.

'You know better than that! What is wrong with you, Mark? I have not seen nor heard from him in over twenty years.' She wrenched her arm from his grasp. 'And if I had, he would not ask about Deborah, because he doesn't know she exists!'

Tears of anger and frustration were streaking her cheeks now. 'Hear me, Mark! This is the last time I will ever, ever discuss this subject with you. I'm going to bed.'

'Don't walk out while I'm talking to you!' He lunged for her, but she sidestepped him and raced, still limping, into the bedroom, slammed the door shut and locked it.

Mark was after her in a flash, kicking at the oak door, hitting it with his shoulder. 'You open this door! Claire, open it or I swear I'll knock it down.'

'If you do that I will call the police.' Claire was trembling but her voice was calm. 'They would probably be curious about how I got the bruises all over my body. Did I mention that you cracked a rib this time?'

Mark continued to batter on the door.

'I'm not bluffing, Mark. I'll do it. I'm sure the *Washington Post* would have a field day with the story: President's special envoy to the Middle East arrested at his home.'

'You wouldn't dare.' But he stopped his attempt to break open the door. 'Too much is at stake.'

'Don't test me.'

Mark and Claire stood on either side of the bedroom door, both breathing hard. Finally, Mark took a step away, his face distorted in frustration and rage.

'Don't sleep too soundly tonight.' He spoke softly, almost in a whisper, but every word came through the thick wood. 'This isn't over, Claire. Not by a long shot.'

And Claire knew that he spoke the truth.

Four

Claire was fragile but gaining strength each day. With Mark away in the Middle East, she had allowed herself to sleep deeply without the ever-present fear that he would come home and find something to be angry about. She had worked from home all week, to avoid questions about her injuries. She had been relieved this morning when she saw that the bruises, which had stained her face, were mostly gone. The marks on her body were disappearing too.

Her heart? That would take longer to heal.

She pushed herself hard as she jogged along Beachside Avenue, past houses of another era, each one grander than the one before. She ran past the inlets where the tide pushed and frothed as it was pulled out to sea. How long had it been since she felt safe, really safe, she asked herself as she ran. The blare of a car horn jolted her out of her musings.

'Are you trying to get yourself *killed*, lady?'

'Sorry, sorry!' she called after the car as it swerved around her and sped away. She slowed to a walk, her heart pounding, the good feelings slipping away. A reminder, she thought, determined to stay on her guard from now on. The world can be at its most dangerous when you're feeling safe.

Martel was a French-style bistro plonked right on the line where Westport met Southport. When you walked through the etched-glass doors, you could imagine you were in Paris.

Marty, the larger-than-life owner, knew his patrons well.

Claire, Sasha, Julia and Paulina had been having lunch there most Saturdays since the doors opened, and always enjoyed being there.

Claire had showered quickly after her run and slipped into cream trousers and a cashmere sweater. A low-slung belt and a cropped leather jacket, the same turquoise colour as her eyes, completed the outfit. It was simple but striking.

'Where were you last Saturday?' Marty, the owner, greeted her like a lost love. She was his favourite.

'I picked up a little bug, but I'm fine now. I missed you too, Marty.' Her quick kiss on the cheek put the smile back on his face. 'Am I the first to arrive?'

Marty gestured to the back room. 'They've

been back there for an hour with their heads together. Plotting the overthrow of the government is my guess.'

Claire hurried towards the back room and slid into her usual place next to Sasha in the big corner booth. The others were already halfway through a carafe of the special house wine, which Marty kept for his favourites. 'Did you have breakfast here?' she asked, air-kissing her three friends.

'Having it now,' Paulina said, pouring Claire a hefty glass.

'Marty tells me you are up to something,' Claire remarked.

'We're celebrating!' Sasha answered.

Claire raised her glass. 'What's the occasion?'

'That you're here, of course.' Sasha said. 'Last Saturday was deadly, right ladies?' The three friends clinked glasses and toasted Claire. 'Marty sulked. And without you we were so depressed we all ordered healthy meals.'

'You didn't!' Claire felt that warm rush of happiness that always came over her when she was with these women. Friends, especially women friends, gave life something extra. She wondered if men knew what they were missing. 'Don't tell me you had salads!'

'Worse!' Paulina exclaimed. She had the body of a swimsuit model and the wit of Joan Rivers. She wore her jet-black hair short and spiky, and could be as funny as the writers of the comedy shows she oversaw for a television network. 'We *shared* salads!'

'It was hell! But you're here now, and all's right with the world.' Julia lovingly cut a large slab of rich pâté, plopped it on a plate and pushed it towards Claire. Julia was the chef at Gumbo, the hotspot just off Park Avenue on 83rd Street in Manhattan. She and her partner, Alexa, had opened it five years ago. They specialised in food from Julia's hometown of New Orleans.

Julia had an ongoing love affair with food. She had been raised in a city where eating was a religion, and not enjoying food was a sin. Gathering her flaming red hair into a ponytail, as though preparing for battle, she tore off a large chunk of bread for Claire and one for herself. 'I think I'll torture myself and just sit here and watch you eat that, Claire, and not gain an ounce! It's very hard being the friend of someone who stays slim whatever she eats.'

Claire ate with gusto, and moaned with delight, 'It's perfection!'

Julia did the same. 'See. I just put on a pound and you look just the same. One day soon I won't be able to wear clothes, even those fabulous rags you pick out for me at Gilda. I'll have to be upholstered, like a chair.'

'Stop it,' laughed Paulina. 'You are beautiful, Julia.'

'And don't worry,' Claire said, taking a sip of the wine. 'Curves are back!'

'In that case . . .' Julia helped herself to another slice of the gourmet pâté.

Claire looked at Sasha who had been somewhat quiet. 'You all right, Sash?'

'Of course I am. Just speechless at all this pigging out.' Sasha signalled for Marty, and continued, 'We missed you on the train this week, Claire.'

Sasha reached over and gently squeezed Claire's hand, just as Marty arrived at the table.

'I see you're all happy now the band is back together.' The other women always insisted he had a crush on Claire, which was probably true. 'Glad to have you back, pretty lady,' he now murmured, looking at her.

'Thanks, Marty. The place looks great!'

'So, ladies, what's your pleasure?'

Sasha topped up Claire's wine glass. 'You know what we like to eat, Marty. You choose. Just bring more wine, please.'

*

Lunch had lasted until three o'clock. Claire and Sasha lingered over their espressos after the other women had gone off for their usual Saturday activities. The good feelings Claire had felt on her run had begun to return, surrounded as she was by the warmth of her friends. But Sasha, usually the life of the party, had been quiet all through lunch. Claire studied her. 'So what's going on with you?'

'I'm worried about you.' Sasha added another cube of sugar to her coffee.

'You didn't say anything to the others?'

'Claire, they're not blind. We've all been friends for ever. I would expect that they know. Wouldn't you know if something was going on with one of them?'

'I suppose.'

'They're just nicer than I am, and keep their mouths shut. But they're worried too.' Another cube of sugar went into her cup. Sasha was nervous and trying not to show it. 'Any word from Mark?'

'Not a word. He usually calls every morning, whatever time zone he's in.' Claire forced a smile. 'But I know he's all right. If he so much as sneezed, the press corps would have it on the front page of the *Wall Street Journal*.'

24

'I'm not worried about Mark, and you know it.'

Claire leaned back, staring at her hands. All week she had tried to push Mark's warning from her mind. 'Don't sleep too soundly,' he had said. 'This isn't over.'

'Do you have any idea what sets him off? Is it really just that he wants you to quit working?' Sasha tried not to look at her friend's wounded arm.

Claire took a sip of her coffee, remembering Mark's questions about Deborah's birth father. 'No,' she lied. 'No idea.'

'When is he back?'

'Tonight, late. It's okay. We'll talk things through.'

Sasha was ready to cry out with frustration. 'What is the matter with you, Claire? You need to see a lawyer. Get some sort of restraining order.'

'You know I can't do that! The newspapers—'

Sasha cut her off, her voice rising. 'To hell with the newspapers! Your life is at stake.'

'There's nothing I can do right now, Sasha. Believe me, I would if I could!' Claire was crying now. 'I'm trapped.'

Marty suddenly loomed over the table, a

worried look on his face. 'Everything okay here?'

'Fine, Marty, thanks. Just, you know, missing Deborah. Her birthday was last week.' Claire slipped out of the booth and grabbed her bag. 'I've got to get to the cleaners before they close at four. Marty, lunch was more than wonderful.' She blew Sasha a kiss and headed for the door. 'I'll see you on the train Monday.'

It was a full five minutes before Sasha could bring herself to move from the table.

Five

Claire guided her sleek navy blue Audi into a parking space behind Green Earth Cleaners. As usual, hers was the only car in the small car park that was reserved for employees and delivery vans. It meant entering the dry-cleaners through the back door, and making her way through racks of plastic-wrapped garments, but she preferred that to the Saturday bustle of the car park at the front.

'Mummy, are you still there?' Deborah's voice came through the car's built-in telephone system.

'Just parking. So tell me more about your performance for the college. Were you nervous?'

'At first. But once I started to play, I just got lost in the music. I played the Rach, masterfully I might add, and then Mozart, a sonata, and finally I finished off with a little Bach.'

Claire couldn't help but laugh. 'A little Bach? Only you would be so at home with that mighty music that you call it little. Are you happy there, my Deborah? Do you really love London?'

'Soooo much. I miss you and Daddy, of course, but this is where I want to be for now. Is he back from Cairo yet?'

'Tonight,' Claire said, trying to keep the dread from her voice. 'Has he called you?'

'No call, but he sent me about ten over-the-top birthday presents. You know how he is.'

Claire forced herself to sound casual. 'Yes. Yes, I do know how he is. So I'll call you next Saturday?'

'Yep! Oh, and thanks for all your birthday goodies. The clothes are gorgeous, of course, but that book, the David Dubal, how did you get your hands on that?'

'I can't tell you all my secrets.'

'I read the Horowitz piece three times – my favourite pianist. You always know what will really thrill me.'

'That's what we moms do.'

'You do it better than most. Take care, Mums.'

'I will, sweetheart. Don't waste a moment of this wonderful time over there worrying about me.'

'Same to you! I'm twenty-one now and completely an adult.'

'Bye, Granny.' Claire laughed. She was about to ring off, when her daughter stopped her.

'Wait! Wait! I forgot to tell you. The most

amazing thing happened at that concert I went to at the Albert Hall, on my birthday.'

Claire had to smile. She loved her daughter's passion for life. Everything was *amazing* to her.

'Well, first of all, how I got the tickets. They just turned up in my mailbox, inside a birthday card. Two tickets to this concert that was completely sold out for ever!'

'What a great gift. Who were they from?'

'I don't know. There was no name on the card. It was probably Dad though, don't you think?'

'I don't know. Maybe. So what happened at the concert? Someone drop a cymbal?'

'No. The conductor, this Maestro Connelly, introduced a new piece, a rhapsody he had written, and guess what it was called?'

'I can't guess. Tell me.'

'*Rhapsody for Claire*. It said it right there in the programme.'

'So I have my own theme song now. Like *Gone With the Wind*.'

'It was a pretty awesome piece of music. Kind of sad, kind of romantic. And he played brilliantly. I'm going to learn it, and play it for you when you come visit in July.'

'I can't wait to hear it. Now you must let me go, or the cleaner will be closed, and your father will have no clean shirts.'

'Horrors! For lack of a clean shirt, Middle East peace never happened. Go, go. Love you.'

'Love you back.' Claire pushed the button to disconnect and just sat for a moment, smiling in spite of everything. How lovely to have a daughter. No matter what she'd given up to give Deborah a wonderful life, it had all been worth it. Mark had been a good father. No matter how bad things had become between the two of them lately, he had kept Deborah out of it.

She released the boot lock of her car so she wouldn't have to wrestle with the shirts later, got out, and, as usual left her keys on the dash-board of the car. The back door of the cleaners had scarcely closed behind Claire, when a very large four by four with blacked-out windows coasted into the lot and parked close, too close, to Claire's car.

Five minutes later, Claire emerged with an armload of plastic-covered shirts on hangers. She stopped dead in her tracks, looked around, unable at first to take in what she was seeing. Her car was gone. She had parked right here, she knew she had.

'Hey, can I help you with that?' A youngish man, with dark curly hair, was leaning against the four by four. 'That's quite a load. I hope you're not walking.' Smiling he grabbed the hangers that were threatening to slide out of her arms onto the ground.

'No. I mean, I drove. My car . . . it was right here five minutes ago.'

The man made a show of looking around. 'I just pulled in, but there was no car here. Were you with someone? Maybe they moved it.'

'No. I was alone. This is crazy.'

'How could someone just drive away with your car? It takes time to jump an engine.'

Claire was kicking herself. 'I left my keys in the car. Dear God, I'm a fool.'

'Don't beat yourself up. It's easy enough to make a mistake. All it takes is once, I guess. You should call the police. Do you have a phone?'

'In the car. Naturally.' She made a face.

'Mine is at home. Looks like we're two of a kind. Hop in. I'll run you down to the station.'

Claire looked at him now for the first time. Something, some instinct, was raising alarm bells in her mind. She took a step back. 'Have we met? You look familiar.'

'I don't think so. I'd remember. Hop in.'

Claire stared at the man, trying to place him, her discomfort growing by the second. 'Thanks, but I'm going back inside the shop to call.' She moved to the open back door of the car, and began gathering up her dry-cleaning.

It happened with lightning speed. The man lifted her off her feet, swept her into the car, and slammed the door.

Claire's heart was pounding at twice the normal rate, and the ringing in her ears was deafening. But the sound was not so loud that she couldn't hear the unmistakable, bone-chilling sound of the doors locking.

She tried to pull the door open but it was securely locked. She pounded on the blacked-out partition between the driver and the back seat. There was no response.

Now she felt the car being put into gear, the lurch as it rolled over the speed bump and out of the car park. Claire was screaming for help now, pounding on the windows, but no one heard her. The car picked up speed, throwing her back against the leather seat.

Mark, she thought, and with the most chilling clarity. Mark is behind this.

Six

Claire had lost all sense of time and direction. During those first terrifying moments after she was taken, each nerve, every instinct in her body, had been on full alert.

Because of her daily jogging, she knew every corner of Westport. She forced herself to focus, to follow the route he was taking. She listened to the traffic noise, but this giant car seemed to be almost soundproof. She listened harder. She needed to know where this man was taking her, so she could plan her escape.

The driver seemed to be repeating the same pattern over and over, and with a sinking feeling Claire realised what was happening. He was driving in circles to confuse her. And he had certainly succeeded.

They drove for what seemed like an hour but it could have been minutes. Claire cursed herself for not putting on a watch this morning. The car had begun to pick up speed. Highway. They were on a highway. She listened carefully. No trucks. That much she could tell. So it couldn't be route 95. The Merritt, maybe. She couldn't be sure. And with all the twists and turns she had no idea if they were heading north or south. Damn!

She began to shiver and her mouth felt dry as a desert. Panic. She knew the symptoms well and fought them as best she could. She leaned back on the seat and took slow, deep breaths, her mind a jumble of thoughts. Mark. Was he just trying to frighten her? Or was Sasha right? Was she in danger? He had a hair-trigger temper, yes. But he loved her and adored Deborah. He wouldn't dare . . . or would he?

She never should have threatened to call the police. She had known as soon as the words were spoken that she had crossed a line. Why hadn't she listened to Sasha, got away from him somehow? Whatever love they once had was gone. But there was Deborah. A girl needed a father.

Stop it, she told herself. Stop finding excuses for him. When, she wondered, had she turned into this passive person, too frightened to stand up for herself, too weak to leave a dangerous relationship?

Claire forced herself to push away the knowledge that Mark Saunders was capable of just about anything – wonderful or terrible. The man had everything: intellect, good looks, brilliant education, charm, even a great sense of humour. Everything but self-control.

But he had not been like this during most of their twenty-year marriage. He had been loving, playful even. And he worshipped his adopted daughter and had been a great father to her. So what was it? What had happened to change him? Why had he suddenly become obsessed with the man who fathered Deborah?

Walker. She rarely allowed herself to think of him, of how they once were. They had just six months together, but it had felt like a passion that would last until the day the world ended. Even after more than twenty years, she remembered everything: how his eyes would crinkle before he laughed, how he knew what she would say before she did. And, of course, she remembered how it felt to be loved by him. No matter how she tried to shut her mind to the memory, if she closed her eyes she could almost feel his hands on her body.

Then he was gone. He just disappeared.

The note said it had all been a mistake, but it hadn't been, not for her. Neither was the child, his child she was carrying. She had never considered adoption, or abortion. This part of him would live, would thrive and be loved, as Claire had loved Walker. And still did, if truth be told. She knew she was in love with a memory.

She had met Mark when Deborah was an infant. She was a single mom doing three jobs, determined that Deborah would have the best life that love and money could provide. She had begun working at Gilda when she was still pregnant, at night she did telephone sales for a magazine publisher. When it was too late to make calls she would design and create one-of-a-kind hair ornaments and fancy bows that she sold on Lexington Avenue outside Bloomingdale's.

Claire was tireless back then. Deborah was thriving in the best nursery in New York City, and already showing a musical talent that was a bit alarming to her mother, who couldn't sing a tune.

Mark had come into Gilda to buy a gift for his current girlfriend. Claire had been busy with another client. He had taken one look at her, and told the other staff that he would wait. He left the store that day with no gift, but a promise from a reluctant Claire to have dinner with him that night. She told him she had a daughter and didn't date, but Mark Saunders had a way of getting what he wanted. Then and now.

His courtship of her had been like something out of a fairy tale. Claire knew that it was his kindness to her daughter that caused her to open her heart and let him in. He was funny and handsome and powerful: a heady mix. Over time she grew to love him. True, it wasn't the kind of passion she'd had with Walker, yet it was real and strong and, she had thought, plenty to build a life on.

When she had accepted his proposal of marriage, when they made the agreement about Deborah, she swore to herself that she would put Walker completely out of her mind and heart. She owed Mark that. And she had done it; shut him out. There was just one reminder she couldn't avoid. Deborah had her father's eyes and, like his, they crinkled just before she laughed, signalling the delight to come.

Sometimes, when she looked at her daughter, she would have to force the memory of Walker away. Shut her mind to the love she had seen in those eyes that first time they had been together. It hadn't been awkward or shameful, just a celebration of a forever love that didn't last.

Stop it! Think of nothing, she told herself. Save energy. Close your eyes and breathe. She needed to be ready when they got to wherever they were going. She would be. She was going to be the woman she used to be, before the violence began. She was strong and she could run like the wind. She would get away. She closed her eyes and took more deep breaths.

Claire awoke with a start to the sound of gravel crunching under the tyres. She'd fallen asleep! How was that possible? The big four by four was slowing down. We're here, she thought, wherever here is.

She heard the dull click of the locks being released, and in an instant she had thrown open the door, leapt to the ground and started running, arms pumping, long legs stretching out across a great lawn. She was practically flying when she glimpsed a path through a stand of birch trees, and headed for it. Claire knew the man would be after her, but he'd better be Usain Bolt if he expected to catch her.

The sound confused her. It wasn't the footfalls of the driver racing after her, but tyres on gravel. She risked a glance over her shoulder. The big car was leaving, following the driveway back down the hill. And there was no one else coming after her, at least as far as the eye could see. But she kept running towards the path, slowing a bit. She needed to be careful now.

Once she reached the cover of the trees, and made sure that no one was following her, Claire slowed to a walk, searching the horizon for something, anything.

She heard a rush of water, waves breaking. She was near water. The ocean . . . she was near the ocean. She could smell it. One step more and she was able to make out stone breakwaters jutting out into the greenish water. The waves seemed gentle. It was the Sound. Long Island Sound. That she was sure of. She listened for some clue, a sign of human life, but there was nothing. Only the screech of gulls, the rush of the incoming tide, and the pounding of her own heart.

Seven

Deborah Saunders hurtled down Devonshire Street, her long sandy curls tossed and tangled by the wind. There had been a late-afternoon shower of rain, so there were puddles to splash in, and splash she did.

She was tall and lean like her mother, but instead of Claire's turquoise eyes hers were hazel, flecked with green and gold. Deborah was lithe like a colt, and full of life.

She screeched to a halt in front of a pair of handsome double doors and began fumbling for her keys.

Her room-mate, Mavis, followed more slowly, lugging a cello, yet still arriving in plenty of time to open the doors before Deborah. Mavis couldn't help laughing at her friend. Deborah was, as usual, scurrying about the pavement, trying to gather up the sheet music that had scattered to the four winds when she'd dropped her backpack, again as usual.

'Do you New Yorkers ever *walk* anywhere?'

Mavis asked, stooping to prevent an expensive musical score from turning into pulp.

'Not when we're excited,' Deborah said, shaking the water off a Mozart sonata, and stuffing it messily into her bag.

'Which is every minute of every day, if you are an example.'

'You Brits are too laid-back by half,' Deborah said, pouncing upon one particular folder of music, cradling it to her with reverence. 'How can you not be filled with joy every minute, just being here in London? I mean, look at the light!'

'I do love being here, Deb. But I guess the English are not the sort to leap about,' Mavis laughed. 'It could also be because I've been carrying a giant fiddle around with me since I was six.'

Deborah held the door so Mavis could wrestle her cello through it and into the lift. 'See you upstairs,' Deborah called as she bounded up the stairs two at a time, the precious folder clutched to her heart. The flat was everything Deborah had dreamed of when she got on the plane to London. Cramped, noisy, quirky and thrillingly her own. She had dreamed of study-ng at the Royal Academy for as long as she could remember, probably ever since her mother had begun letting slip tiny details about her own time in London.

Maddeningly, the Claire-Sphinx, as she and her friends called her exotic mother, rarely gave up details about that time. If you asked her about studying at the Royal Academy of Art, she would say things like, 'It was special but a long time ago.'

Sometimes, right out of the blue, Claire would start talking about London in a way that made you see it . . . about rain showers that just happened and then went away; how a little corner of the city could become your very own place; and how there was a time, when she was in London, that Claire believed any dream could come true.

Deborah had had her own dream since she first sat down at a piano. To make it come true, she had practised when she would rather have been hanging out with her best friends. Astonishingly, they were the children of her mom's best friends. She was a student at the Juilliard School, and when her friends went to Cancun in Mexico for spring break, she flew to Ohio to take an intensive course with famous pianists.

The news that she had been accepted at the Royal Academy of Music to study piano performance made it worth every sleepover, every party, she had ever missed. She had insisted on coming to London alone. She wanted to find her own flat, make her own way. Her dad had not been keen; in fact, he had been adamantly opposed to her coming to London at all. He had fought tooth and nail to stop her from enrolling in the Royal Academy.

Her mother, on the other hand, had been fiercely supportive of her. 'She's earned the right to make her own choices,' Claire had insisted and, despite immense pressure from Deborah's dad, she never wavered, nor deferred to him, as she usually did.

Mavis took her cello from its case, propped it up in its stand, and sat on the piano bench next to Deborah. 'Tell me again how you got your hands on this piece of music?'

Deborah was studying the composition, her fingers moving unconsciously as she read each bar. 'I stole it, of course.'

'When we heard it at the Albert Hall it was the very first performance. The piece hasn't even been published yet.'

'Which is why,' Deborah said, continuing her study of the score, 'I had to pinch it.'

'Seriously?'

'Seriously. Although I prefer the term *borrowed*. But I just had to have it. You heard it. It's such a magnificent composition, so filled with passion and longing.'

'So you just walked into Maestro Connelly's office and took it? You know you could get expelled.'

'I would never risk that. You know Renny from composition class? He played first bassoon at the concert?'

'The storky fellow?'

'Be nice. You need to be tall to play the bassoon. Anyway, I asked him if I could have a look at *Rhapsody for Claire*, and he said yes.'

'Just like that, he handed you a piece of music that's still a work in progress?'

'Well, I did have to promise to meet him for tea when I return it tomorrow.'

'You are shameless.'

'Isn't it great! I've never been shameless before, and I quite like it. Anyway, I'm doing it for a good cause. I'm going to learn the rhapsody and play it for Mom when she comes for my term-end concert in July. *Rhapsody for Claire*, performed by piano prodigy, Deborah Saunders.'

'Very cool. All right, I approve this crime.'

Claire pulled out her computer and a small keyboard and began to copy the piece.

'If you're going to get that thing copied by

tea-time tomorrow, you'll have to pull an all-nighter,' Mavis said, standing up. 'I'll brew up a pot of tea that'll keep you awake until St George's Day.'

It was late in London, and Mavis had long since gone to bed. Deborah was so engrossed in her work that, when her phone rang, she actually jumped. She checked caller ID: it said, HOME. 'Hi, Mom, what's up?'

'It's me, Deborah.'

'Dad! When did you get home from Cairo?'

'Just a little while ago.'

'So did you make the world safe for democracy?'

'Not yet, I'm afraid. That may take a few more centuries. So tell me about your classes.'

Ten minutes later they were still talking about nothing. Her father, who usually was a *just the facts, ma'am* kind of guy, had asked more questions on this call than he had in the last ten years.

Mavis wandered sleepily out of the bedroom and mouthed, 'Everything all right?'

Deborah shrugged and mouthed back, 'Dad.' She made the hand gesture that shows someone is talking and talking, and rolled her eyes.

Finally she cut in. 'Dad, it's great talking to

45

you, but I've still got a lot of work to do before class tomorrow. Thanks for calling, and thanks again for all the birthday presents. I didn't even know you knew what a metronome was.'

'I'm a man of many talents,' he said. 'I'll let you get back to it.'

'Okay Dad, love you.' She started to end the call but he stopped her.

'I was wondering . . . when did you last talk to your mother?'

'Mom? Tonight. Well, my tonight, your afternoon. Why?'

'No reason. Just wondered.' There was a long pause. 'Talk about anything special?'

'Dad, you sound weird.' There was something about this call that was bothering her. 'Is everything all right with Mom?'

'Of course. She's just fine. Don't pay any attention to me. I'm just a little jet-lagged, I guess. Get back to whatever you were doing. Night.'

Mark hung up the phone quickly, and cursed himself for his clumsiness. He poured himself another drink and prowled around the long room, feeling as jumpy as a caged lion.

He needed to find out how much Claire had told their daughter about their personal problems. He suspected she was telling everyone she ran into about things that should be private between a man and his wife. He checked his watch. Soon, he thought. Soon things will be settled once and for all.

Eight

Claire was huddled in a little shelter she had found down at the water's edge. She was shivering, but not from fear. She was past that now, her panic replaced by a steely determination to survive at all costs. She was cold. She had checked the shoreline and could see no sign of life. She had to clear her mind, to think. Where was she? And, more importantly, why was she here?

'Mrs Saunders! Claire!'

The voice, a woman's voice, was coming from up the hill, near where Claire had jumped from the four by four. She kept very still, making herself as small as possible in the corner of the old shelter.

'Claire! My dear child, where are you? You must be freezing.' The voice was closer now, a little out of breath. Silently, Claire got to her feet, reached up for one of the wooden oars that had been stored in the roof of the hut, and held it at the ready. It would make a clumsy but effective weapon. Who was this woman?

She sounded so . . . kind. Not at all like someone coming to cut her throat. It had to be a trap.

'Forgive me for not being there to greet you. There was an emergency. Where are you, my dear? Don't be frightened. Please.'

'Don't come any closer!' Claire hardly knew her own voice. 'I warn you.' A twig snapped on the other side of the shelter, and Claire whirled around.

'I've brought a shawl for you.'

Claire cocked the oar over her shoulder like a baseball bat.

'Oh, there you are.' The woman stopped when she saw Claire. 'My goodness, that looks heavy.'

Claire just stared. Standing before her, showing no fear whatever, was a pink-cheeked middle-aged woman dressed in a ruby-red, almost pink, nun's habit.

'Take this,' the woman said, holding out a bright pink shawl. 'I'm Sister Mary Theresa. And of course I know all about you. Claire Saunders. You are as lovely as I was told.'

Claire's mind seemed to be shutting down. 'Who are you? What is this place? Why was I brought here?' She was still holding the oar at the ready.

'So many questions. Why don't you put that down, dear? You're liable to get a splinter. It's been out here all winter.'

Despite the plight she was in, Claire saw something in this woman that just washed her fear away. Slowly, almost without realising, she lowered the oar. She still kept her distance, but her breathing was slowly returning to normal. 'Why did you have me kidnapped?'

'Kidnapped? We didn't think of it like that. But, of course, I can see how you might.'

Claire felt as if she were Alice in Wonderland, and had just tumbled down the rabbit hole and run into the Mad Hatter dressed as a pink nun. 'You said *us*. Who is us? What do you want with me?'

Sister Mary Theresa crossed quickly to Claire and wrapped the shawl around her trembling shoulders. 'Come with me up to the house. I've got a fire going, and once you have a hot cup of tea we will explain everything.'

'I don't want tea and I'm not going anywhere with you! I want an explanation and I want it now. And who is *we*?'

'You know, my dear,' said the unflappable nun, 'if you had been this firm defending yourself from the person who is really a danger to you, perhaps you would not have those bruises

50

on your wrist. Now follow me. Your friends should be here by now.'

'Friends? What friends?'

'They do think the world of you, my dear. They had hoped to be here before you, but it took longer than they thought to stash your car.'

Claire just stared.

Sister Mary Theresa giggled. 'Listen to me. *Stashed*. I think Mother Superior is right, I've been watching too many episodes of *LA Law*.' She turned and headed back up the hill. 'Come along now.'

And, despite her confusion and fear, Claire followed.

Nine

Mark sat in one of the wine-coloured leather club chairs in his study, staring gloomily at the blazing fire. The bottle of Oban malt whisky on the coffee table was lying on its side, empty.

Mark rarely had more than one drink. He thought drinking in excess was a sign of weakness, and he detested weakness in himself and others. Yet here he sat, drinking alone in his own home, having made a crucial error with his daughter. He finished the last of the Scotch in his glass.

Where the hell was she? Claire knew he was coming home tonight. Seven o'clock on a Saturday night and no sign of her, not even a phone call. She needed to be taught a lesson. He got up suddenly, filled with an anger made worse by lack of someone to share it with. He scooped up the bottle and headed into the kitchen, where he buried it deep in the rubbish bin.

He grabbed a bottle of beer and checked his watch. Nearly eight. He hadn't expected her to be here when he got back this afternoon. Saturday afternoon was *her* time. Time to be with girl-friends, run errands, maybe take a run. But this? Unacceptable! It's those friends of hers; he knew that they had got at her. She was with them now, he was sure. Gossiping about him.

He still wasn't over the fact that Claire had insisted on allowing their daughter to go off to London on her own. She rarely defied him like that, and he thought he knew why she wanted Deborah in London without his supervision. Well, she was coming home, that was for sure. Once he and Claire had a meeting of the minds tonight, he was pulling Deborah out of that school.

He took a long drink of the beer. When did Claire become like this? They used to be happy. The perfect family. From the moment he had seen her at Gilda, he knew he had to have her. Claire, with her dazzling good looks and unique sense of style, and the exquisite Deborah, with her one-of-a-kind musical gift; they fitted perfectly with Mark, and his place in the government and the world. Having his family with him at a state dinner, or a function anywhere in the world, gave added lustre to his image. Not that he didn't love them for themselves, above and beyond the way they boosted his career.

But in the last few years the way the family worked had changed. Deborah was twenty-one now and a free spirit. And Claire . . . well, Claire was no longer to be trusted. But he knew what needed to be done. She must be brought into line.

He put a dirty plate in the sink with a clank and began searching in the drawer of the little roll-top desk that Claire used for her household accounts. He tore through the neatly ordered papers, letting them land where they fell, until finally he found what he was looking for. He pulled out a leather-bound address book, searched through it for a number and dialled. His jaw twitched with irritation as he listened to the rings.

A man picked up after four rings. 'Hello.'

'Jeff, how are you? Mark here.'

'Sorry. Mark? Is there a last name or is this a quiz?' Jeff was pleasant, but clearly didn't recognise his voice.

Mark's irritation was rising by the second. 'Mark Saunders.'

'Ahhh. Yes.' Jeff's tone had changed abruptly, its warmth gone. 'What can I do for you?'

'You can ask Sasha what she's done with my wife. It's after eight and she's not here.'

'Why don't you call Claire and ask her?'

'If she was answering her phone, I wouldn't be bothering you.'

Silence on the other end of the line. Mark was instantly on guard. What was going on here? Jeff had always been friendly. 'Jeff?'

'I'm here.' Jeff's tone was flat. Noncommittal.

'Is Claire there?' It was impossible for Jeff not to detect the edge in his voice, but Mark didn't care. 'If she is, I want to talk to her now!'

'Hey man, calm down. You're off base.'

Jeff was being as cold as ice. Someone had been telling Jeff lies about him, Mark was sure. 'Put her on the phone!'

But, instead of a reply, Mark heard the distinctive sound of a telephone being hung up. In a rage, he hurled the phone across the kitchen. He knew it. She'd been talking! Mark grabbed his beer and his car keys, and headed for the door that led from the kitchen into the big four-car garage.

The space where Claire's car should have been felt like a personal insult. He slid into his enormous black Mercedes, backed out of the garage, and roared down the driveway and through the gates. He would find his wife and, when he did, he would make sure this sort of thing never, ever happened again.

Ten

Claire, still wrapped in the pink shawl, kept her distance from the colourful nun as they approached the door of what could only be described as a gothic fortress. The castle-like structure came complete with turrets, leaded-glass windows, pointed arches, stone gargoyles and a pair of carved oak doors large enough to admit a tank. In the fading light it looked beautiful but a bit ominous.

'What is this place?' Claire was still on alert, ready to run if she needed to.

Sister Mary Theresa studied the building thoughtfully. 'It is different things to different people, I suppose. It was built by a wealthy man around 1910, as a gift to his lady love.'

'And what is it for you?'

'That's a good question. I suppose to me this is a place where people can learn all they need to know about living as well as dying.'

Claire took a step backwards, wary again.

'Don't pay any attention to me, my dear. I tend towards the dramatic. When the gentleman who built the place was close to dying, he became concerned about his place in the Kingdom of Heaven. So he left the house, the outbuildings and the land to the church. This is where I live and do my work.'

The doors opened with a great creaking of hinges. Sasha, followed closely by Paulina and Julia, ran out and threw their arms around a very confused Claire. All three of her friends tried to hug her at once, and their words poured out in a jumble.

'Are you all right?'

'Are you cold? We're so sorry we weren't here to meet you when you first arrived.'

'I know you must have been frightened, but we didn't know what else to do.'

Claire just stared at them. 'You did this? You did this to me?'

'You wouldn't do anything to help yourself, so we had to,' Julia said.

'Kidnap me? You had to kidnap me? Why? Why on earth would you put me through that?' She pulled herself away from her friends, her eyes blazing. 'I thought I was about to be murdered!'

'So did we.' Sasha was shaking her. 'So did we all. And we had to get you to a place where Mark couldn't find you. He's a powerful man.'

'You had no right! This is my life and I can handle it.'

'That might have been true a few years ago. But something has happened to you, Claire. You're cowed. You've lost the ability to fight for yourself. It happens to women when they are being constantly abused.' Sasha tried to wipe away her tears and Claire's. 'Abusers don't stop being abusers, unless someone makes them stop,' she added.

Paulina's voice was gentle. 'You have been powerless to stop Mark from hurting you, so we stepped in to get you to safety.'

Claire caught her breath as she saw the worried looks on Julia's and Paulina's faces. She turned to Sasha. 'You told them! You promised me you wouldn't say anything.'

'I didn't tell them!'

Claire wrenched herself away from Sasha's embrace. Paulina put a protective arm around Sasha. 'For heaven's sake, Claire, do you think we needed to be told? We ride the train to Manhattan together every morning. We'd have to be blind not to notice the sudden use of make-up, the long-sleeved shirts in the middle of July.'

'This can't be happening. Poor Mark! This could ruin everything he's trying to do.'

'Yes indeed. Poor, poor Mark! It must be so tiring for him to come home after a day of being idolised in Washington and then have to beat the bejesus out of his wife!' Sasha was so angry she was shouting. 'Remind me to send him a sympathy card! What I'd like to do is run over him with my car!'

'Enough!' Sister Mary Theresa, who had been taking all this in, took charge. Her tone was soft, but there was power behind her words. 'Nothing is going to be solved if you all just stand out here shouting at one another.'

The women stopped talking, taken aback by the authority in her voice.

'Inside, all of you. Go into my study. I'll bring some tea and then we will sit quietly and speak like adults. Until then, no talking. Not a word.'

And the women found it impossible not to obey her.

The four friends drank their tea in silence. Claire sat a little apart from the others, closer to the fire.

They were in a large room with a vaulted ceiling and walls covered in wood panelling. One entire wall was taken up by a massive but graceful fireplace. Above the mantelpiece hung a very large, painted emblem of Sister Mary

Theresa's order. It looked as if it had been painted quickly.

Sasha was studying it and Sister Mary Theresa explained. 'There's a carving under there of the lady for whom the house was built. She's naked and lying with her man friend. It's a fine piece of art, but we felt we should cover it up.'

'Sister,' Julia said, studying the nun, 'you certainly are different from the nuns who used to smack me on the knuckles with a ruler when I was at school. They would have torn down the whole fireplace with their bare hands. *If thine eye offends thee, pluck it out,*' she quoted, playing up her New Orleans accent.

'Well, at least the good sisters, who I am sure were well-intentioned, taught you your Matthew,' the nun said. 'Or was it Mark? Both of those dear saints were very keen on removing any body part that offended.'

Julia laughed aloud, and the others joined in, and somehow the terrible tension that had filled the room began to melt away. Claire still sat apart, but even she began to relax a bit.

Sister Mary Theresa began collecting the empty teacups, placing them on a large oval tray. 'Isn't it amazing how a cup of tea, and staying quiet, can change one's ideas?' She crossed to where Claire was sitting staring at the fire. 'Julia believes her teachers behaved roughly towards her. Perhaps they did. But I can assure her they did what they did because they cared deeply for her.

'The same might be said for your friends here. The way they went about getting you out of harm's way was extreme. And there's no question it caused you great distress. But I do know this complex scheme was born out of love for you, and a deep fear that your life is in danger.'

The nun hoisted the large tray to her shoulder with the ease of an expert waiter and spoke to Claire's anxious friends. 'I remind you all that, no matter what decision Claire makes, you must go with it. Paulina dear, ring the bell when you are finished here, and I will come back.'

'Yes, Aunt Mary.'

Claire's head whipped around as Sister Mary Theresa kissed Paulina on the head.

'I do wish you would consider letting your hair grow. I did so love plaiting it,' she said. And then she was gone.

Claire spoke almost without wanting to. 'That's your aunt?'

'Afraid so; my mother's older sister.'

'She's . . . I don't know . . . amazing.'

'Isn't she? And she's always on at me about my hair. Does she really expect me to manage a bunch of comedy writers in pigtails?'

'I think it would be a good look for you.' Claire managed a smile, and within seconds they were all on their feet, hugging Claire, hugging each other, laughing and crying at the same time.

Eleven

Sasha and Jeff Granger lived in a sprawling log house perched on the shore of the Saugatuck River.

Jeff was a patent lawyer. He was on the raised, screened-in porch that jutted out over the river when he heard the car. It was tearing down River Road and turning, tyres shrieking, into his driveway.

'What the hell?' He went into the house and down the corridor that led to the front entrance. Before he could get there, someone was pounding on the door and shouting.

'Claire! Damn it! Get out here! I know you're in there.'

Jeff pulled open the door to find Mark, coatless and reeking of booze, panting like a prizefighter. 'What do you want?'

'I want to talk to my wife. Now!'

'Claire isn't here, and if she were I wouldn't let you near her. Not in the state you're in.'

Mark, who at six foot two was half a head

taller than Jeff, started to push his way into the house. Jeff would not be moved.

'Claire! We're going home!' Mark shouted.

'You're either drunk or out of your mind. Now get off my property or I'll have you arrested for trespassing,' Jeff threatened.

Mark tried to push the smaller man out of the way, but Jeff was stronger than he looked. 'I wouldn't put your hands on me, if I were you, Mr Special Advisor. In case you've forgotten, I'm a lawyer.'

'No court in America would convict a man for trying to find his wife,' Mark yelled.

'You may have been spending too much time in the Middle East, Saunders. In this country, it's against the law to use your wife as a punch bag.'

Mark took a swing at Jeff, which he blocked. Just then a low growl echoed down the hall, and an over-sized Rottweiler appeared at Jeff's side. The dog did not seem to like the vibes he was sensing, and he put his head down and growled again.

Mark froze where he was, staring at the dog, which stared back at him.

Jeff laced his fingers through the dog's collar. 'Now that I think of it, Rocky here might be able to handle this without my having to call the cops. Get out of here before I let him loose.'

The dog growled again with menace.

Mark turned and headed back to his car. He'd left the car running with the lights on and the driver's door hanging open. He slid into the seat and slammed the door. Feeling brave there in the safety of his car, he lowered his window a bit. 'We're not done, you and I, Granger. Count on it.'

Jeff locked the door and went into the room that he used as his office, grabbed his phone and began texting.

Mark just showed up half drunk looking for Claire. Is she safe?

A few moments lapsed before he received Sasha's reply.

For now. Got 2 convince her to stay.

The guy's out of control. Don't let her go home. Gd lk. LU

Sasha texted right back.

Gonna try. LU2

Jeff put the phone in his pocket and went out onto the porch. Looking at the river always cleared his mind. He petted Rocky, who was sitting next to him, on guard. What the hell had happened to that guy? Was he snapping under the pressure of his job? If so then, no matter where Claire was hidden, Mark would find her.

Twelve

'You guys are crazy! I mean, stealing my car? Having me taken to a convent?'

Sasha drew Claire down next her onto the worn, overstuffed sofa. 'Desperate times require desperate measures. We need to talk.'

The other women pulled up chairs and drew together in a small circle in the vast room.

'Sasha, I told you I could handle Mark.'

'You've been telling me that for over a year, Claire. I know you think you can, but you can't.'

Julia chimed in. 'He's got you so scared that you aren't the person we've always known.'

'You're pretending, kiddo.' Paulina took her hands. 'Not just to us, to yourself. Seriously, do you feel safe with Mark? Can you be yourself with him? Are you happy? Is this the kind of relationship you want to be a model for Deborah?'

Claire started to protest but stopped in mid-sentence. If she said yes to any of those questions she'd be lying. She knew it and they knew it.

'Okay, I know that you were trying to take care of me. But, despite your lack of faith in me, I am capable of making my own decisions. Tell me what you want to tell me, and then take me home. Mark was due back this afternoon. He'll be crazy mad that I just disappeared without a word.'

No one said anything. They just looked at Claire, waiting for her to realise what she had just said.

'*Crazy mad*,' Sasha said. 'I rest my case. Our case.'

'All right. He *is* a little bit crazy sometimes. But what is it you want me to do? Stay here? Become a nun? I have a job, a daughter. I have a life.'

'Your job can wait. You haven't taken a holiday for five years. Your daughter is in London. As for your so-called life, I don't think you have one any more.'

Claire stopped listening to what Sasha was saying. It was too painful to absorb all at once.

'There's something I want you to see,' Sasha said, squeezing Claire's hand. 'Paulina, was Sister Mary Theresa able to arrange everything I asked for?'

Paulina smiled. 'What do you think? Give Aunt Mary a task, and it's done by the time you finish speaking.' She pulled aside a curtain to reveal a large screen TV with a DVD player, and turned to Claire. 'Your pal Sasha, producer, director of more award-winning television commercials than you can count, has put together a little show for you. Get the lights, Julia.'

'What is this?' Claire was getting edgy.

'You'll see. You'll recognise some of this.' Sasha hit 'play' on the remote, and the screen was filled with the image of a small stage set up under a banner that read NEAR AND FAR BENEFIT.

Claire, dressed as Captain Hook, swaggered her way onto the stage, followed by Sasha as Peter Pan, Paulina as Wendy and, bringing up the rear, Julia as the Crocodile. She was having great difficulty with her tail.

They were greeted with applause and began to sing – or rather tried to sing – a version of 'Never Smile at a Crocodile'. However, they were laughing so hard at Julia's struggle to keep from tripping over her tail, that the only distinct words were the Crocodile's tick-tock, tick-tock.

Claire couldn't help but smile. Soon all four of them were singing along with the DVD and laughing almost as hard as they had that night.

Their on-screen performance finished to thunderous applause.

A charming, happy-go-lucky Claire stepped to the microphone, and addressed the audience saying, 'If you enjoyed that as much as we did, please pledge whatever you can to keep Near and Far helping families here in Westport and anywhere else there is a need.'

The camera panned to the audience, where a vastly different Mark Saunders was standing throwing bank-notes onto the stage and urging the other members of the audience to do the same. He was relaxed and happy and obviously proud of his wife.

Soon the quartet was being pelted with money, which they stuffed into the now-untied tail of Julia's crocodile. 'That was five years ago,' Sasha said, pausing the tape.

'I had forgotten how wonderfully awful we were,' Claire said.

'We haven't forgotten, Claire.' It was Paulina this time, crowding in next to Claire on the sofa, putting an arm around her. 'Play last year's benefit, Sash.'

Sasha pressed 'play' and they were back at the same place, with different decorations. In the background could be heard music from *The Mikado* as some other Westporters made fools of themselves for charity. The camera, however, was focused on a table for eight. The four friends and their husbands, doing their best to be festive. It was obviously an effort.

Mark sat stony-faced, and Claire chattered nervously, trying to appear normal. Dance music began to play and an MC called the crowd to the dance floor. Three of the husbands jumped up and led their wives to the floor. Mark remained in his chair.

The moment they were alone at the table, he grabbed Claire's wrist and started scolding her. The sound wasn't clear, but the rage on his face was. Claire tried to wrench herself away from him but he was too strong. He gave her wrist a twist, got up from the table and left. Claire sat there for a long moment trying to settle her face, discreetly nursing her injured wrist, and looking around to see if anyone had noticed.

Sasha stopped the DVD, freezing the frame on Claire's misery. Claire couldn't take her eyes off her image on the screen.

'I didn't capture this scene on purpose, Claire, I want you to know that.' Sasha told her. 'My video guy had taken a cigarette break and left the camera focused on our table. I only watched this a few weeks ago. I cried when I saw it.'

'I didn't cry,' Paulina said. 'I signed up for a kick-boxing class so I could take that man down if he ever lays a hand on you again, Claire.'

'That's not helpful, Paulie,' Julia said.

'Sorry. But I'll do it, I swear,' Paulina promised.

'The thing is, Claire,' Julia said, kneeling at her feet, 'you don't have the strength to get away from him. That's what happens to women who are battered. They can't bear what's happening to them, so they convince themselves it's not so bad. But it *is* bad! It's horrible! And it's getting worse.'

'We want you to know –' Sasha paused, twisted around, so Claire had to look her in the eye – 'that if you are not strong enough right now to fight for yourself, we will do it for you until you *are* ready. Please, please let us help you.'

Claire was still transfixed by the misery of her image on the screen. Finally, she turned to her friends. 'All right. What is it you want me to do?'

The women looked at one another, relief obvious on their faces. 'For starters, stay here for a few days. Hang out with Aunt Mary. She's a pretty wise old broad.'

'Mark will be looking for me. You know that,' Claire told them.

'He won't find you. We stashed your car up at the lake,' Paulina explained.

'I'll stay, but just for tonight. And what about Deborah? He'll call her. She'll be frantic!' Claire looked anxious.

'I'm her godmother,' Sasha said. 'I'll take of her.'

'You won't tell her about this, any of it?' Claire asked nervously.

'Of course I won't. If she ever knows, it will be from you.'

'All right,' Claire said.

Paulina pulled a velvet cord, and they all began gathering their things. 'Aunt Mary will be here in a minute. Love you, babe.'

They all gave her hugs, but Claire was simply too numb to respond.

'We will be in touch in the morning. Just sleep, okay? And know you are safe,' Sasha reassured her.

They were almost out of the door, when Claire stopped them. 'That man who brought me here. Who was he?'

'Marty drafted in his brother, Keith. I think Marty's been more worried about you than we have. Love you!' Paulina flashed a smile.

And then they disappeared out through the huge doors and into the darkness, leaving Claire alone in the great hall. She poked the ashes, kindling what was left of the fire. 'They don't know Mark,' she whispered to herself. 'They don't know the kind of power he has. He *will* find me.'

Thirteen

Mark drove home cautiously. The run-in with that vicious dog had cleared his head enough to make him realise that he could not afford to have his car stopped.

After what seemed for ever, he turned off Sasco Creek Road and drove through his own gates. He was too worked up even to feel relief. He could not believe he had put himself in this position. He never drank to excess like this. Jeff, he was sure, would entertain everyone on the train tomorrow morning with tales of Mark Saunders' drunken visit. He'd have the whole carriage laughing about how his crazy dog nearly tore one of the President's key men apart.

He let himself into the house, still kicking himself for going over to the Grangers'. That move was not smart; it was not him. That, and the call to Deborah, had shaken him. What was wrong with him? He was the guy who thought things through, the guy who never asked a question unless he knew what the answer would be.

He checked the answering machine. Nothing.

It was Claire. This was her fault. She was turning him into someone he wasn't. Well, that was going to stop. No more drinking, that's for sure. He could best deal with Claire with a clear head.

He went into his study and sat at his desk thinking things through. After a moment or two he knew what he must do. He unlocked a drawer and took out a throwaway cell phone and a small address book. He found a number and dialled it. The call was answered instantly.

'Yes sir?'

'I have a job for you.'

'At your service.'

'I need you to find someone for me.'

'Consider it done.'

'It's a bit tricky.'

'I specialise in tricky, as you well know. That's why you're calling me.'

'Where are you?'

'Next question.'

'Sorry. I'm not myself tonight. How soon can you be in Connecticut?'

Mark waited, listening to the sound of someone typing fast on a computer keyboard.

'I can be in New York by nine tomorrow morning. I'll call you on this phone when I land.'

'I'll be waiting.'

A click and the call was disconnected. Mark locked the phone and book back in the drawer and, feeling lighter than he had in some time, headed for the shower.

Fourteen

Claire followed Sister Mary Theresa down a dimly lit corridor lined with doors on either side. The nun had a grace about her that made her seem young, and with her habit silently skimming the floor, she appeared to be floating. She opened one of the arched oak doors and entered, beckoning Claire to follow.

It was a small room, furnished with a twin bed in an ancient iron frame, a straight chair and a low chest with two drawers. On the chest stood a jug of water, a glass, and the lamp that gave the room's only light. A colourful hand-made rag rug was spread on the wooden, wide-planked floor. Instead of a wardrobe, several round wooden pegs stuck out from the wall.

'These were the servants' quarters when this was a grand home. I must warn you the heating up here is erratic, but I'll bring more blankets for you.'

'I'll be fine, Sister.'

'I know you will be. Although the comfort level is not what you're used to, here we offer what your beautiful home cannot: safety.'

Claire shuddered. 'I don't know how to thank you for going to all this trouble for me. I just don't think I should . . .' She stopped herself. 'Problem is, I can't think right now.'

'You don't need to think; you need to rest. I've put a nightgown for you, there on the bed. You get changed while I rustle up some blankets.' Claire managed a smile as the nun left the room.

She peeled off her leather jacket with great effort, more tired than she could ever remember. She had just pulled off her sweater when Sister Mary Theresa floated back into the room holding a quilted bed cover.

'Holy Mary, Mother of God!' The Sister spoke without thinking. Her eyes were fixed on Claire's back and shoulders, which bore the scars of many an old battle. Although a week had passed since the last attack, her entire left side was still covered with bruising.

'My dear child, what has he done to you?'

Claire covered herself with the nightgown and hung her head, fighting tears. 'I provoke him.'

Sister Mary Theresa's touch was gentle as she

lifted Claire's chin, but her voice was filled with outrage. 'Do not hang your head, ever. This is not your fault! Someone has made you think you deserve to be beaten, but that is not true.'

'There are things you don't know.' Claire was still trying to keep from crying. 'I've not been a good wife . . .' She sank onto the bed, too exhausted in mind and body to stop the tears from coming.

Sister Mary Theresa sat next to her, helping her into the nightgown. 'Look at me, dear.'

'I tried. I really tried. I did everything I could think of to make Mark happy. But maybe there was always part of me that was somewhere else. I think he sensed that. And that's why he hurts me. Because I hurt him.'

Sister did not speak until Claire lifted her tear-stained face to her. 'People feel the way they feel, Claire. We cannot always control our thoughts and our feelings. That's part of being human. What we *can* control is our behaviour. Our words and our deeds – they are what matter.'

'I loved Mark when we were married. I love him now. But not in the right way.'

'I see. Well, actually, I don't see.' Sister Mary Theresa found a white handkerchief somewhere in her habit, and gave it to Claire. 'I wasn't aware there was a right and a wrong way to love. I've been taught that the very act of loving is in itself perfect.'

'I loved Mark but not enough, don't you understand? It was not like I loved . . .' the name came out in a whisper. 'Walker . . . Walker Kennedy.' When she said his name, a name unspoken for so many years, it was as though a dam had burst and the words started pouring from her in a torrent.

'I don't think I can find the words to explain what it was like, Sister. Think of any cliché you've heard about love: at first sight, passionate, soulmates, one person in two bodies. That was what it was like for Walker and me. Sadly, "star-crossed" also applies. We had everything, and then nothing. It was over. He was gone. Love was gone.'

'Would you like to tell me about it?'

'I don't want to, but I think I have to. I've kept it all bottled up inside so many years: twenty-two, to be exact. Maybe, if I say it all, I can escape from him once and for all; put the memory away in a place where it can't hurt me or hurt Mark.'

'Then by all means, say it all.'

Claire curled up on the narrow bed, lost in another time. 'I know this sounds crazy, but it makes me happy just to hear his name, to say it out loud after so many years. Walker Kennedy. It sounds like music. It's a story I've never told anyone, not even Sasha. It's a story so terrible and wonderful that, if it were known, life would never be the same for me or Mark. But, most importantly, for my darling Deborah.'

Fifteen

Sasha, Paulina and Julia were sipping wine on the screened-in porch, listening to the Saugatuck River burble and complain as the low tide pulled it back towards the Sound. Connecticut evenings in early spring were chilly, but the splendour of a full moon over water made the cold bearable. The women were lined up on the sofa, three across, feet on the coffee table, wrapped in blankets.

Paulina sighed, looking at the moon. 'We look like three desperate housewives on the deck of a cruise ship. All we need is Claire here for this to be paradise.'

'Do you think she'll stay there, where she's safe, at least for a day or two?' Julia was munching on some nuts she just happened to have in her giant handbag. She offered them to the others. 'You have to admit, we were a little out of our minds to try to pull this off.'

'It's a good thing we did it when we did it. You heard Jeff. Mark was over here looking for her, raging like a lunatic.' Sasha topped up their wine glasses. 'I wish Jeff *had* let the dog go after him.'

'I wish he could guard Claire twenty-four/ seven,' Julia said, pushing her wine out of reach. 'But since he can't, we need to do it.' She offered her friends another nut.

'You know, Julia,' Paulina said, 'if you pulled a leg of lamb out of that handbag of yours, I wouldn't bat an eyelid.'

'People need nourishment in time of stress.'

'Quite right,' Sasha agreed, helping herself to another. 'Now let's go over everything before this wine takes effect. We need to make sure there are no loose ends. Paulina, are you sure no one saw you take Claire's car?'

'Only the snatcher,' she answered, rolling her eyes. 'I parked out at the front, and walked around, and there was Marty's brother, leaning against the car, doing his best to look like he'd just stepped out of *The Sopranos*. I didn't dare make eye contact with him. Claire's keys were on the console, just as you said they would be.'

'I've been telling Claire for years that leaving her keys in the car was a bad idea,' Sasha said. 'How a woman as smart as she is can be so blind to danger is beyond me.'

'Maybe it's because she's so kind herself – she can't get her head around the fact that not everyone is like her. Anyway, once I got the car out of the lot, I headed up to the lake, going about two miles an hour so no one would notice me. I put it in the barn like we planned. Julia picked me up in her truck and we headed back to meet you. I certainly hope my life of crime is over,' Paulina said, getting up and stretching. Then she added, 'Obeying the speed limit is a nightmare.'

Sasha turned to Julia. 'You fixed her phone so she can't be traced?'

'Like I told Claire, I followed Paulie into the back lot and ran over that phone with my truck, crushing it completely.'

'So, no loose ends?' Sasha raised a brow.

'Well, there is one.' Both women stared at Julia. 'I got a text a little while ago. Marty's brother Keith is freaking out because he's been driving around with Mark Saunders' shirts in his car. About twenty-five of them.'

'Oh lord,' Paulina said.

'He's afraid he'll be arrested for stealing shirts. Seriously.'

Sasha had to giggle. 'He had no problem kidnapping a woman in broad daylight, but he draws the line at shirt-napping?'

'Maybe it's a federal offence.' Paulina was laughing now. 'They've got some crazy laws on the books. He may have broken section two, article eight of the dry-cleaning act.'

And in seconds they were all helpless with laughter.

'I needed that,' Sasha said, wiping tears from her eyes, serious now. 'Okay, *Mark*. We must deal with Mark before he makes the rounds of all of our homes issuing threats.'

'Good plan,' Julia said. 'I can't promise Alexa won't greet him with a baseball bat if he so much as walks up on the porch.'

'I'll call him,' Sasha said, reaching for her cell phone.

'Now?' Paulina checked her watch. 'It's two in the morning.'

Sasha was already dialling. 'If he's not up, he should be. His wife is missing.'

Mark picked up on the first ring. 'Mark Saunders.'

'Hi, Mark, it's Sasha. Jeff said you stopped by tonight.' She switched on the speakerphone so the others could listen.

'Where is she? Where is Claire?'

'She's not there?'

'If she were here I would not have been out looking for her. I'm frantic with worry.'

Sasha rolled her eyes at the other women. 'I'm sure you are, Mark. I was at a meeting for

Near and Far. Claire didn't show up there either. I have no idea where she is.'

Mark, careful not to lose control again, switched on the charm. 'Come on, Sash, you four gals don't comb your hair without checking with each other.'

Paulina made a face, mouthing *gals*.

Sasha gave back as good as she was given, turning on a little charm of her own. 'You *guys* don't know how to make friends, so you'll never understand how it is with us *gals*.'

Julia gave her a thumbs-up.

'Well, now I'm worried about Claire,' Sasha said. 'Did you check your answering machine? Look for a note? Maybe she texted you?'

Mark was having trouble pretending to be friendly. 'I'm not totally without a brain, Sasha. Of course I did, plus I've checked the hospitals, even called the police to see if there had been any accidents. There weren't. So I just assumed she was with you.'

'We had lunch together around noon, just like always. But she left a little after three to go to the dry-cleaners. She hadn't been able to go there since she went to Paris, and was very concerned that you would need shirts.'

The women looked everywhere but at one another.

'The dry-cleaner?' Mark was pacing now. 'Either she didn't go, or she went somewhere afterwards, because I don't have a damned shirt in my closet.'

Sasha turned her back on the other women, fearing they would make each other laugh again. 'That's tough, Mark. But that's all I can tell you. Hey, call me the minute she comes home, will you? I won't sleep a wink. Night.'

'Wait!'

'Yes Mark?'

'Today at lunch. How did she seem?'

'I'm not sure what you mean?'

'Did she say anything . . . about us, me, I mean?'

It was hard for Sasha not to let her dislike of the man show in her voice. 'Just the usual: how great you are, how lucky she is to be married to you. Frankly, Mark, it makes us all kind of sick when she talks like that.'

'Why is that?'

'Well, you know, the rest of us bitch about our lives, and there she sits, married to Mr Perfect. We're all just jealous, I guess. Gotta go.' She hung up the phone carefully.

'Do you think he bought that?' Julia asked.

'Hard to say.' Sasha was pensive. 'The guy lies for a living.'

*

87

Over on Sasco Creek, Mark sat in his study, looking at the phone. She knows something, he muttered under his breath, thinking it through. The throwaway phone on the desk rang sharply. Mark answered it before the first ring was finished. 'Mark Saunders.'

'I got your text, giving me particulars. The cell-phone number you gave me is not giving off a signal.'

'I thought you could track an iPhone anywhere.'

'Not if it's been destroyed.'

'Damn!'

'Don't give up so easily. Does her car have a tracking system?'

'Of course.'

'Text me her licence-plate number and we'll find it. My flight is boarding. See you in the morning.'

Mark checked a file in his desk and texted the licence number. He ended the call, headed for the bedroom and fell asleep instantly, satisfied that it was only a matter of time before Claire was home. With him.

Sixteen

'We met in a London taxi.' Claire was sitting on the bed, so lost in her memory that she was only faintly aware of Sister Mary Theresa. 'It was pouring rain, and I was late for class, so I flagged down a cab. Just as I was getting in through one door, I looked up to see this guy getting in through the other. Well, not just a guy. He was drop-dead gorgeous, with sandy hair and hazel eyes that crinkled up around the edges when he smiled at me; as a bonus, he had this hunky body.'

She stopped, realising who she was speaking to. 'Sorry, Sister.'

'I believe I understand the word. I wasn't born a nun, you know. Go on.'

'I had forgotten my umbrella, so I was soaked to the skin and late for my class. He was soaked, too, so we decided to share the cab. I was shivering from the cold, and he reached over and rubbed my hands to warm them. A shock, literally like a bolt of electricity, went through my body. I think . . . well, I know he felt the same thing.

'By the time we got to the Royal Academy of Art, where I was studying, we were talking as though we'd known each other for ever. We both still had so many things to say that we agreed to meet for dinner that night at the Queen's Head and Artichoke. It's an adorable little pub near the Royal Academy of Music.'

'Queen's Head and Artichoke. Certainly sounds adorable. So he was English?'

'He was born in London, but he had spent most of his life in New York. His father was an American. A lawyer for the FBI in the Organised Crime Division. His mother was English. We talked and talked, and when the pub was ready to close we still had so much to say that we decided to walk. So we walked and walked, and we didn't stop walking until the sun came up.'

Claire was clearly revived by the memories. Sister Mary Theresa barely moved, not wanting to break the mood.

'I should be embarrassed to tell you this, Sister, but I'm not, because it was inevitable. We skipped class that day, went to the room I was renting, packed up my things, and by tea time I had moved into his tiny two-room apartment over a Chinese restaurant.'

Claire laughed, remembering. 'It was a squeeze for sure. Half the living room was taken up by an enormous grand piano. I couldn't imagine how he got it up to the second floor, but I soon found out that if Walker made up his mind, there was nothing he couldn't do.'

'He was a musician?' Sister Mary Theresa asked.

'He was studying composition at the Academy, but he was already a brilliant pianist. So we'd both go off to class in the morning, and then race home . . . because five hours away from one another felt like for ever.'

Claire had to stop to gather herself, as the memories triggered long-hidden emotions. After a moment or two, she went on.

'The owners of the restaurant downstairs sort of adopted us and gave us dinner most nights. We'd have a Chinese feast and then I'd curl up in a corner of the living room to work on my sketches, and he would go to the piano. First he would play whatever composition he was working on at the Academy, and we'd talk about what had inspired him, and what he was trying to accomplish. Really, it was thrilling to be part of that.

'He, of course, would pore over my drawings, and listen to me talk about art. And finally, when we were both done with work for the next day's classes, I got to choose a composer. Rachmaninoff, I'd say, and he would play Rachmaninoff. And I had to guess what it was – a sonata, a rhapsody, an étude. I got a first-class musical education just by falling in love.'

Sister Mary Theresa couldn't help but notice how Claire's face was changing as she fell back into her memories, and into another time. She seemed younger, even more lovely, if that was possible. The sadness written on her face when she arrived tonight was fading away.

'To this day,' Claire said, 'when I pass a Chinese restaurant, I can't help but smile, no matter how badly things turned out. Those five months were the happiest of my life. Except when Deborah, my daughter, was born.'

'What a beautiful name. The original Deborah was a prophetess and a warrior. What is your Deborah like?'

'Certainly a warrior. Nothing fazes her. She's a girl just bubbling over with energy and curiosity and joy.' Claire thought about whether or not to say more, then decided to go for it. 'She's also a brilliant musician, a pianist.'

'I see.' Sister Mary Theresa was careful now about what she said. 'Is that a coincidence or an inherited talent?'

'She's Walker's child. Although he's never seen her. But she's Mark's daughter. He adopted her when she was not quite two. She has never known another father, and she has no idea that Walker even exists.'

'My goodness, child, you certainly have been carrying a lot in your heart. One thing I have learned over the years is that secrets are tricky. One way or another, they are usually revealed.'

'This one won't be. Ever. That was my agreement with Mark when he adopted her,' Claire said.

'She was a child then. Now she's a woman. Do you think it's wise to continue the pretence?'

'Nothing would be gained by her knowing. Mark has his faults, but he loves Deborah. I think one of the things that makes him behave the way he does is the fear that her birth father will come back, and that he will lose her love.'

'Has he ever hurt her?'

'Never! He would never ever abuse her! I told you he adores her.'

'Did you ever imagine he would abuse you?'

'Oh, Sister, I can't even let myself think of such a thing. But if he lifted a hand against her, she would not put up with it. Like Deborah in the Bible, she would be a warrior.'

'Are you not a warrior, too? The girl you just

described to me, the young woman who dared to love at first sight, certainly seemed like one.'

'I've changed.'

'Would it help to tell me about the ending? Certain things, emotions we hold inside for too long, have a way of chewing us up, of breaking the heart.'

Claire studied the older woman. 'You seem to know more about life than I would have imagined. How did you become so wise, living away from the world like this?'

Sister Mary Theresa smiled. 'As I said earlier, I was not born here. But my life before is between me and my confessor. Now, tell me what happened to you and Walker.'

'It was the middle of June. Walker's father was working in New York, on a big trial of some famous Mafia boss. I can't remember the name. Anyway, he called Walker and asked if he could come home at once. He wanted him to be at the trial.'

'Did you go with him?'

'I had another week of classes, so no, I didn't go, even though Walker wanted me to. I had already planned to come back to the States, and – this is silly, I know, but we had seen this old movie at a film festival: *An Affair to Remember*.'

'Cary Grant and Deborah Kerr, I remember

it well. A three-hanky movie, to be sure. They were to meet at the top of the Empire State building—'

'If their love lasted. So we decided that on the Fourth of July we would meet there at noon. He would have arranged everything. A Justice of the Peace would marry us right there; then we'd celebrate by watching the fireworks on the East River and live happily ever after.'

Claire, who was beyond tears by now, got up and poured herself a glass of water. She stood looking out of the room's only window at the peaceful Sound below. The gentle colours of dawn were creeping across the great lawn.

'He didn't come?'

'He didn't come. I never saw him again.'

'Dear girl.' Sister Mary Theresa went and stood near Claire, looking thoughtfully out through the window with her. 'Surely you searched for him? In the movie there had been an accident.'

'There was no accident, although at first I thought there must have been. I didn't know where his family lived and I had no way of finding out. People didn't have mobile phones or iPads in those days. Because of his high-profile work, his father's phone number was not in the phone book. But I had been following the trial in the papers, so I knew when Mr Kennedy would be at the court-house. When he arrived for the first day of the trial, I was waiting for him on the court-house steps.

'I called to him, and all of a sudden the policemen who were guarding him were swarming around me, questioning me. But Mr Kennedy moved them aside, and said, "You're Claire, aren't you?" It was as though he had been expecting me.'

'I was frantic, asking if Walker was sick, or in the hospital, or worse. He told me Walker knew I would find him, and he handed me an envelope and left. Just walked up the court-house steps and into the court-house with his bodyguards.'

Sister Mary Theresa sighed and sank onto the bed. 'Sometimes life is so hard. I ask the Lord about it all the time. Why? Why?'

Claire sat next to her. 'Does he ever answer?'

'In His way. My faith teaches me that life on earth is not perfect. Life thereafter is sublime. It's a matter of faith, I suppose, and I, like everyone else on this earth, have sometimes found that answer to be not good enough. But it's the only one I have.'

'It was the typical Dear John letter. He would always love me but we were just not meant to be. Have a nice life, he wrote. Have a nice life.'

Sister took her hand. 'Did you ever try to find him?'

'Of course I did. I was like a crazy person. But he was just gone, vanished. So I never got to share the surprise I was saving for the Empire State Building. He never knew I was going to have his baby.'

There was nothing left to say. Claire curled up in the narrow bed, and Sister Mary Theresa tucked the quilted cover around her, so she was in a little cocoon of warmth.

'Sleep now, dear girl. I must be at my work in an hour. I have patients to see. But I will come to see you at lunch. Sister Margaret is right down the hall, and will bring food or anything else you need. Try not to think any more. You are in a place of healing.'

'There's a hospital here?' Claire was already drifting off to sleep.

'We Sisters run a hospice here. We help people learn how to die well. It is my wish that we may help you learn how to live.'

Claire was asleep before the door had closed.

Seventeen

Morning brought with it grey skies and a biting wind. Mark, however, didn't notice the weather as he focused on the task at hand. He was pacing around the parking lot in front of Green Earth Cleaners, when Mr Park opened the doors at eight a.m. sharp. Mark was careful to be on his best behaviour. He put on a politician's smile.

'Good morning! Mark Saunders. I don't think we've met.'

'No, I would have remembered,' Mr Park said politely. 'Of course I have had the great good fortune to know Mrs Saunders for many years. You know, sir, when I was a boy in Korea, my father always was telling me that if you choose the right woman to wed, half of what you need to do in life will be done. You, Mr Saunders, have chosen well.'

Mark pushed down a sudden flare of anger. Another fan of Claire who believed she walked on water. Was he the only person in Westport who could see the truth of who she was? Did no one else see the lies, the betrayal? But the smile never left his face. 'I'm a lucky man, no question about that. I'm just on my way home from the airport and thought I'd save her a trip and pick up my own shirts for a change.'

In Mark's line of work, lying was called diplomacy.

'I believe your wife picked everything up yesterday afternoon, but I'll be happy to check.' He hurried back inside. Mark followed, watching as the man checked his records. 'No, nothing left. She took everything.'

'I'm not surprised. As you say, she's a wonder.' Mark made as if to turn away, then stopped. 'Do you happen to remember about what time she was here?'

'Same time as always: three fifteen. We close at four on Saturdays.'

'Thanks. Next time if I want to help out, I'll know I have to get here before that.'

Mark was heading out the door when Mr Park, nervous in the presence of the great man, chatted on. 'I hear the back door open on Saturday. The plastic rattles and I know it's Mrs Saunders coming. Nobody else uses that door.'

'The back door? Why does she do that?'

'Busy lady. Smart lady.' He laughed. 'Front parking lot on Saturday is like a party. She has better things to do than gossip. Please give her my regards, Mr Saunders.'

'Sure will.' Mark left the shop. He had more questions, but to ask them would attract attention. It wouldn't do for him to be going around Westport tracking down his wife.

The back door? Who was she meeting back there? He wanted to drive around and have a look, but he could see Mr Park watching him through the window, so he got into his car and drove away.

He didn't need to be doing this anyway, he reminded himself. Someone was on the way who was an expert at finding people who didn't want to be found.

Eighteen

It was midday in London, but Deborah had been at the piano for several hours. She had managed to scan *Rhapsody for Claire* into her computer before she went to bed last night. It was morning before she put her head on the pillow. She hadn't slept well because the phone call from her father had troubled her.

Her dad had not been himself for a while now. When she thought about it, things had begun to change soon after she had committed to becoming a concert pianist, and had begun to study at Juilliard. She had hoped he would be proud of her for her talent and work ethic. Sadly, his reaction had been just the opposite. He hadn't even come to her senior solo concert at Alice Tully Hall. Despite the full house, it had been hard to hide her disappointment when he did not show up.

Deborah forced these concerns from her mind and went back to the music. She was determined to master the complex piece by the time her mother came for her concert in June.

However, learning this would not be easy. She spanked the piano keys in frustration: so many moods, such a mix of colours and tone. She got up and stretched, wriggled her fingers, sank into her favourite yoga pose, the lotus, and closed her eyes. Her mother had taught her that when stress was greatest, it was best to close your eyes, breathe deeply and take your mind to another place. Breathe, she told herself. Breathe. In through your nose and out through your mouth. Let your mind take a holiday.

Something was wrong between her parents. She'd known it for a couple of years now. They both tried to hide their feelings but, even though they never exchanged a cross word when she was there, she could feel the tension between them. Her father was only partly there, not fully. And her funny, happy, wonderful mother had a sadness about her that hadn't been there before.

Mavis wandered in from her bedroom, wearing her ridiculous pink flannel pyjamas patterned with white and black sheep. 'Is lying underneath the piano a new way to absorb music?'

'I might do better down here than I was doing at the keyboard. That piece is a nightmare.'

Mavis joined her under the piano. 'Your guilt at becoming a music thief is blocking your talent.'

'I like the term "bandit" better than "thief", if you don't mind. It sounds more romantic. Did I wake you up banging on the piano?'

'I needed to get up anyway. I have a ticket for the lunchtime concert at St Martin-in-the-Fields.'

'Aren't you a little late for that?'

'I'll make it by the interval.' Mavis yawned and stretched. 'You know, it's very nice under here. We should do this more often.'

'I think my parents should get a divorce.'

'What?' Mavis propped herself up on an elbow and studied her friend's face. 'I thought they were the perfect couple.'

'They are perfect, just not together. It suddenly came to me as I was lying here. I bet they're staying together because of me.'

Mavis scrambled out from under the piano. 'I'm getting out from under here, before I imagine Prince Harry is going to join me for the concert today.' She went to the bedroom to change, muttering to herself. 'Note to self: a life of crime brings madness.'

Deborah lay where she was for a moment, lost in thought, then scrambled up, found her phone and dialled. Nothing happened. She was puzzled.

Mavis popped out of the bedroom, heading

for the shower down the hall, and saw the puzzled look on her room-mate's face. 'Everything okay?'

'First Dad calls in the middle of the night, sounding weird. And now Mom's phone is dead. When I left for London, she told me she'd never turn her phone off; that I could reach her day or night.'

'What are you thinking?'

'I'm not thinking, I know. Something is very wrong at home.'

Nineteen

Claire woke to the sound of angels singing. At least, that's how it sounded to her. She wasn't sure exactly what music it was, but she knew it was some sort of heavenly choral piece – a hymn, maybe.

Deborah would know. She'd name the composer, the time period in which it had been written, and would probably be able to sing along with the Sisters who were *somewhere* in this vast building, celebrating Mass. The very sound of the music seemed to wash away some of the pain in Claire's body and mind.

She had no idea what time it was and she didn't care. It was hard to imagine that the events of the previous day and night had happened to her, and were not something she had dreamed. It had been real, she knew. Her friends had actually arranged for her to be kidnapped and brought to a convent on Long Island Sound. And she had told a complete stranger – a pink nun, for heaven's sake – the story of her life; hers and Walker's. For the very first time since Deborah had been born, she had told someone how her dear, dear daughter had come by her musical talent. And she felt better for having done it.

Claire had kept that story, and those deep feelings, bottled up inside for so long that they had become little more than a constant ache, like a nagging back pain. Now that she'd spoken the words, she felt free to remember the sheer joy of it. The way it felt to be madly, giddily happy and in love. She smiled at the memory; smiling with real happiness felt strange, like a skill she must learn again.

She got out of bed and looked out of the high little window at the Sound. The water was churning under grey skies, yet the world shone to her – the way London had looked that first night with Walker. She vowed she would say his name aloud sometimes, just to hear the music of it. Claire laughed out loud. Twelve hours in a convent and she was already taking a vow. Suddenly she was hungry. She quickly pulled on her clothes, which someone had cleaned and then placed neatly on the chair. She opened the door to go in search of Sister Margaret, and there was Sister Mary Theresa floating down the corridor, carrying a small tray.

The meal was simple. Bread, homemade, of

course; freshly churned butter, and a bowl of fresh sliced peaches. Not just any peach – the juiciest, most delicious that Claire had ever tasted.

'We have our own orchard, but it's too early in the season for our crop. If I can keep the other sisters from eating them all before they leave the tree, we freeze them and enjoy them year-round.'

'I had no idea you could freeze a peach. But then I've learned quite a bit in the past twenty-four hours.'

'Have you?' The Sister was kind, but she had those eyes that seemed to bore into you. 'Tell me about that.'

'It's hard to explain . . . but I think I was putting so much energy into keeping secrets, I was unable to see what is real in my own life, and what isn't.'

'But now you do?'

'I see enough to know that I need to stop lying to myself about Mark. It's not the pressure of his job and it's not my fault that he hits me. He can't control his temper.'

'You've learned all that in one night? I must say that – in my experience – wisdom does not come suddenly; rather it comes gradually, over time.'

'That's just it, Sister. It has come over time. I've known where this would end since the first time Mark raised a hand to me. However, I wouldn't let myself know it, if that makes sense. I couldn't have the life I wanted, the one with Walker, so I made up a perfect life with Mark, and I clung to it even when I knew it was over. I played my part to the full. So did he, until he just couldn't do it any more.'

'If you are excusing him again, then you've learned nothing.'

'Understanding, not excusing. Those are two very different things. My friends are right. He is a danger to me and I cannot stay with him. I lay in this wonderful little bed this morning, realising that Mark has scarred more than my body. He's torn away so many little pieces of me that I hardly recognise myself.'

'Then stay here. Take some time to find yourself again.'

'He will find me, no matter where I hide. Sister, you cannot comprehend the power he has, what he is capable of. He will never let me go willingly, I know that. So I must find a way to force him to. And I must do it now. If I don't take charge of my life right now, I may never again have the strength or the opportunity.'

The wise nun looked at Claire for a long

moment. 'I think I'm beginning to see signs of the woman your friends described to me. The woman you once were, before this all began. All the same I'm worried. If he is the man you say he is—'

'Oh, he is, Sister. But I have one advantage. I know Mark better than he knows himself. I know how he thinks. And I believe I know a way to make him set me free. You have to trust me.'

'Oh, I do trust you, Claire. It's Mark Saunders I don't trust.'

Twenty

St Mary's by the Sea in Bridgeport was named after a tiny, long demolished chapel that perched on the edge of Long Island Sound in an area known as Black Rock. Benches dot the path that winds for several miles along the shoreline, and on a fine day they are filled with lovers and bird-watchers and fishermen. Today, with the wind whipping, the area was deserted, except for a lone man wearing a baseball cap.

Mark was slouched on a bench staring at the Sound. He pulled up the hood of his North Face fleece, not to shield him from the wind, but to hide his very recognizable face from passers-by.

He watched a jogger coming from the north, running easily. As he drew closer, the man slowed to a walk, checking his pulse, and finally came to a stop near Mark's bench. He leaned on the bench to stretch – first one leg, then the other – as he scanned the horizon for watching eyes.

'What did you find out?' Mark asked, still looking at the water.

The man had short-cropped dark hair, green eyes, and spoke English with no accent. Mark had worked with him on other continents, where he had also spoken the native language with no accent. His country of origin, his age, his real name were all unknowable. Today he was Bill.

'Her phone was purposely destroyed. I found a fragment in the car park behind the dry-cleaner's.'

'The car?'

'The tracking sytém was helpful. It's inside a structure near a little pond in New Hartford, Connecticut, owned by Christopher and Paulina Redford. No sign of a struggle or foul play of any sort.'

'I knew those harpies were involved.' Mark was on his feet. 'I'll crush them for this! What else?'

'I grabbed a sandwich and a beer at your wife's hang-out, Martel. I met a chatty barman there by the name of Keith. He's the owner's brother and he's neither smart nor discreet. He couldn't resist telling me about a job he had Saturday. He made a hundred bucks driving some lady to a convent. Description fits.'

'A convent? Where?'

'I'm sure he would have drawn me a map, but the owner of the place called him into the kitchen. Anyway, he didn't come back, and Marty took over the bar. He tried to find out who I was, and got nothing from me except my all-American smile.'

'Why a convent?'

'Maybe she decided to take the veil.'

'Damn it! That's enough smart remarks. You need to find the place now!'

'And you need to back off. You hired me to do a job and the job will be done. There are one hundred and twenty-two convents and monasteries in the state of Connecticut. If she's in one of them, I'll find her. The real question is: what do you want me to do with her when I do?'

Mark got up and started walking away. 'I'll think about that. By the time you find her, I'll know.'

Twenty-One

The waiting list for Martel's famous Sunday brunch was long, and those waiting to be seated were packed into the side porch drinking Bloody Marys. But Marty didn't notice the fraying nerves of the would-be diners as he huddled in the back room with Sasha, Paulina and Julia.

'What did he look like?'

'Dark hair, about six feet, athletic, sort of ordinary at first glance. But when you really looked at him, dangerous.'

'How much did Keith tell him?'

'I'm not sure. I probably shouldn't have hit him so hard. He was carrying on about his broken nose, and wouldn't tell me anything. He just ran off, out of the back door. It's my fault. I never should have trusted him with something so important.'

'You didn't have many choices, Marty. If it's anyone's fault, it's mine,' Sasha said, filled with worry. 'I missed *something*. I still can't work out how they found her car. Paulie, did your neighbour up at the lake say what the guy she saw looked like?'

'He had a hat pulled down and the collar of his jacket was up.'

'Was there a car parked anywhere on the road?' Julia was so nervous she had eaten an entire bowl of olives.

'No, he must have walked in, like I did. She didn't think anything of it at first. What struck her later was that it was odd seeing a stranger up there at this time of year. So she called me.'

'I think we have to assume it's the same guy,' Marty said, cursing under his breath.

'Agreed. But how did he find the car?' Sasha was nearly beside herself. 'What did we miss?'

Julia jumped up, almost knocking the table over. 'Tracking system!'

'Of course! He tracked the car by its GPS. Stupid, stupid!'

'Look, we're not professionals,' Paulina said, although it was clear that she, too, was blaming herself.

'This guy seems like a pro.' Marty looked worried. 'He's gotta be one of Mark's people.'

'If he found the car, he can find Claire. Anything yet?' Julia asked Paulina, who had been dialling on her phone all the time they had been talking.

'Nothing. No answering machine, no answer.'

'It's a convent. I don't think they have answering machines,' Julia said.

'We've got to get her out of there before this guy finds her.' Sasha headed for the front door, saw the crowd waiting for tables and called the others to follow her. They went into the kitchen and through the back door. She called back to Marty, 'Find your brother. We need to know what he told this guy. Paulina, you drive.'

'With pleasure.'

They crammed into Paulina's Ferrari Four and she roared out of the car park.

Sasha's phone rang, causing the three women to jump. 'Hello?' She froze, mouthing the name, *Claire*. 'Where are you?' She listened carefully. 'I know exactly where you mean. Stay out of sight, we're on the way.'

'What happened?' Julia asked.

'Paulina, head towards the Merritt. Someone, a man, called the convent saying he was from the fire department and needed to make an emergency inspection.'

'So fast. This guy is good.'

'He may be a professional, but your Aunt Mary hasn't spent all those nights watching repeats of *Law and Order* with her patients for nothing. She didn't fall for it. She told the guy some nonsense and got Claire out of there.'

'Where is she?'

'Claire didn't want to say on a phone line, but I know. Remember that place we went hiking, and had too much wine? We all ended up skinny-dipping in the Aspetuck Reservoir. In the middle of November.'

'How could I forget?' Julia shouted. 'It took me a month to get rid of my cold.'

Paulina put her foot down, and in seconds they were speeding north.

Twenty-Two

Sister Mary Theresa followed the man called Bill out of the convent, chatting in a friendly way. 'Now you're sure the carbon-dioxide level is all right? You certainly gave me a fright when you called. Some of our patients are very ill.'

Bill had a CO_2 detector slung over his shoulder. His manner was polite and professional. 'Someone must have sent in a false report, Sister. I'm very sorry to have violated this holy space.'

'God allows rules to be broken when there is a real need.' Sister Mary Theresa looked up towards heaven, and silently prayed for forgiveness.

'That's good to know. I will leave you to your good works.'

'Thank you. Oh, and I'm sorry to have kept you waiting. We've had a guest staying here and I had to drop her off.'

Bill didn't bat an eyelid. 'I hope you didn't rush back because of me.'

'I didn't have to go far. She likes to run and there's a wonderful trail that runs along the reservoir up in Easton. I'll go back to pick her up in a few hours.'

'Easton? There's some pretty wild country up there.'

'Yes, too wild for me. We Sisters live quiet lives,' she gave him an angelic smile. 'However, I always say, to each her own. Claire will have her run and then be waiting for me at the head of the trail.'

'You've had a busy day, so I'll be on my way.' He slid into his car and drove down the driveway. He was on his phone the moment he was out of sight. How stupid can a person be, he muttered?

At the other end the phone was picked up instantly.

'I know where she is.'

'Good man!'

'So it's decision time. Do you want to handle this or should I?'

'This is my job,' Mark said, a decisive look on his face. 'Pick me up at Stew Leonard's, in the store's car park. It's busy there on Sunday. No one will notice an extra car. I want to be there to see her face when you grab her. After that you will take us back to our lovely home, where we will work out our differences privately.'

'I'll be there soon. Be ready.'

*

118

Sister Mary Theresa watched as Bill drove slowly down the driveway, as if he were in no hurry. The *LA Law* fan knew better. She pulled a phone from the pocket of her habit and dialled a number.

Claire, dressed now in newly bought running clothes, picked up the equally new phone on the first ring. 'Did he come?'

'He was here trying to get in when I got back. He wanted to inspect the place and I encouraged it.'

'So, what do you think?'

'I think your idea is insane. I think we should call the police.'

'And say what? That Mark Saunders, one of the President's best men, is using every tool at his disposal to find his dear wife, who disappeared without a trace? He could talk his way out of that in thirty seconds. He'd say he was worried, suspected foul play.'

'I see your point,' Sister Mary Theresa murmured.

'So did the guy believe what you told him?'

'I think the gentleman who called himself Bill had no trouble believing I was a doddering old nun, too out of touch to know a con when she saw it. You should be expecting him within the hour.'

'I'll be ready.'

'You've been through a lot, Claire. Are you sure you're up to this? It's dangerous.'

'No more dangerous than spending the rest of my life wondering when Mark is going to come for me.'

She looked at her three friends who were huddled around her, with frightened looks on their faces. 'I know him, Sister. He's not going to have someone shoot me or throw me in the reservoir. Whatever he has planned for me, he will want to do it himself.'

'I'll be praying.'

'Me too. I don't know how to thank you for—'

But Sister Mary Theresa had rung off, and was already working the rosary beads in her hands.

The women were sitting round a picnic table, heads together. 'We can't let you do this, Claire,' Julia said.

'It's okay for you all to have me kidnapped, but not for me to try and save myself? I'm doing it,' Claire said with quiet determination. 'If you guys don't feel you can help, I will understand. I think I can do it alone.'

'Like hell you can,' Sasha said, hopping off the bench. 'I'm in.'

'Me, too,' Paulina cried, heading for her car. 'Julia?'

'Did we have lunch? I don't think we had lunch.' The other two dragged her towards Paulina's car. 'Of course I'm in! I just don't see why we have to starve to death in the process.'

'How long do you need, Sash?'

'Three days. But I'll swing it in an hour. You stall; give this guy a run for his money.'

'That you can count on. Good luck.'

Claire's words were lost in the wind as the car sped away, leaving her alone. It was bleak and cold. She began the wait. If this worked, she would be free. If not . . .

She shook off the dark thoughts. She would not allow herself to think of failure. She must do this for herself and for her daughter. Sasha was right. Sister was right. For now, she was the object of Mark's fury. How long would it be before he turned that anger on Deborah?

She could do this. She would think only happy thoughts. She'd think of Walker.

Claire heard the car before she saw it. She crouched down, pretending to tie her running shoe. She forced herself not to notice as the car did a sharp turn into the little car park.

Only after she heard the doors being thrown open, did she allow herself to look up. She barely saw the dark-haired man heading towards her at a trot. All she saw was Mark, standing by the car, looking at her with a little smile on his face.

She didn't have to pretend to be frightened. She was. She turned and ran, ran faster than she ever had, ran as though the hounds of hell were at her heels.

As, in fact, they were.

Twenty-Three

Claire had fallen in love at first sight with the elegant lines of the old stone house she and Mark shared. Today, as she was driven up the long driveway, child-locked into the back seat of a rented car, the place looked sinister.

No one had spoken a word since the man called Bill had finally caught up with her, after she'd stumbled on some roots on the rustic trail. The car stopped under the arch, the lock snapped and her door was opened by the dark-haired man.

'You're quite the runner, Mrs Saunders.'

Claire said nothing, nor did she look at Mark, who was opening the front door. He gave a small nod to the other man who, without a word, got into the car and drove slowly back down the driveway. Claire fought the urge to run after the car, preferring the risk of being with the stranger to what she knew awaited her when she walked into the house with her husband.

'You must be cold. Let's go inside.'

Claire finally forced herself to look at him. So

handsome, she thought; genteel, well-mannered, and so very, very dangerous. She walked past him through the hall and into the gallery. There was no mistaking the sound of the click as the front door was locked behind them.

'Can I get you something to drink? You must be thirsty after your run.'

When Claire didn't respond, he strolled over to the drinks bar, pulled a Perrier from the fridge and offered it to her. She made no move to take it. He opened the bottle and drank deeply, moving in close to her. 'I've been worried about you, Claire. What were you thinking of, running off like that?'

She did not respond.

'Did you really think I wouldn't find you? A convent? Really? If you hid in the Vatican I would find you.'

Still Claire said nothing.

Mark's expression never changed as he hit her hard across the face with the back of his hand. 'It's very rude not to speak when spoken to, Claire.'

A trickle of blood from her nose ran down her face and dropped onto the carpet. Claire looked at the stain as it spread, then back at Mark, still silent.

'You and I need to come to an understanding,

Claire. I can't have you risking everything I have worked my whole life to build, have you running around Westport spreading lies about me.' He struck out blindly, knocking Claire to the floor.

She looked at him for a long moment, then finally spoke. Her tone was calm but intense. 'What lies, Mark? My friends know you hurt me. Is that a lie?'

She tore off her running shirt, exposing the scars and bruises. 'Is this a lie? And this?'

'It's your fault, not mine, Claire. You drive me to it! You drive me mad with your lies!'

'I don't lie to you, only for you. So that no one knows what kind of a monster you really are.'

'Oh yes, St Claire of Westport. Everyone in this town – hell, the whole world – thinks you're the perfect wife; the loyal, supportive companion to the great man. They don't know how you sneak around, seeing him, telling him about me, about Deborah. She's my daughter, not his.'

Mark was becoming crazy, kicking out in his anger, causing a lamp to crash onto the floor, just missing Claire's head.

'What are you talking about? Seeing *who?*'

'Do you really think I'm blind? Or stupid? I know all about the two of you.'

Claire tried to crawl to her feet. 'I'm not seeing anyone, Mark. I never have.'

'Don't lie to me! I read the letter, his letter. I know I'm just the poor sucker you tricked into raising your daughter, giving you a perfect life. While you waited for your true love to come back for you.' He spat out the words as if they were a curse.

Claire was on her feet, fearless as she faced him down in his frenzy. 'Have you lost your mind? What letter? Who are you talking about?'

'*Dearest Claire.*'

Mark was quoting something he'd obviously read over and over again. '*I hope you will read this letter through to the end. I don't expect you to forgive me for what I did, for not meeting you that July day but, now that it is safe, I want you to know the reason for it.*'

'Walker.' The intensity in Claire's voice was such that this time Mark took a step away from her. 'Walker wrote a letter to me and you didn't give it to me?'

Mark reached back and grabbed a poker from the stand in front of the fireplace. 'You're not going back to him. You're not leaving me.'

'That's it!! Cut! *Cut!!!* I think we have what we need.'

Both Claire and Mark whirled around at the

sound of Sasha's voice. She stood on the landing holding a video camera. Julia was on Mark in a flash, pulling the poker from his hand, as Paulina put an arm around a numb Claire and led her over to the bar. She searched the little fridge for ice to stop the bleeding from Claire's nose.

'Mark, I think you should know that we caught this entire scene on videotape.' Sasha could barely hide the loathing in her voice.

Mark, for once, was speechless.

Claire, ignoring the blood that still ran down her face, crossed the room to face this man who had terrorised her for the past five years. 'So, here is what's going to happen, Mark. You are to walk out of that door and never come back. You will never speak to me or even approach me. You will give me a divorce. You will stay away from Deborah. Should you break these terms, or if any sudden accident should befall me, a copy of this tape will automatically be sent to every news organisation around the world.'

Claire's friends moved in and the four of them stood shoulder to shoulder, presenting a united front. They were also keeping each other from crumbling as Mark Saunders, one of the most powerful men in the world, stared at them with utter hatred.

Without a word he turned and headed for the door.

They had won. Claire had won. She was free.

'Wait,' Claire said sharply. Her voice stopped Mark, whose hand was already on the door handle. 'My letter? Where is my letter?'

'There's a locked drawer in my study.'

'Key?'

He fished in his pocket and took a small key off a ring and handed it to her. 'I love you, Claire. I love Deborah as if she were my own daughter. Can't you see that? I couldn't stand the thought of losing either one of you.'

The great man suddenly found himself fighting tears. 'I think I'm not well. I think the pressure . . .' His voice trailed off.

'Deborah is your daughter, Mark. Still. We will work something out in time. If you get help.'

She looked into the eyes of this man she knew so well but clearly didn't know at all. 'Goodbye.'

And she turned away. But she did not take a step until she heard the sound of Mark's car heading down the driveway. And out of her life.

Twenty-Four

It was late June. Claire, dressed in khaki slacks and a simple white blouse, entered the tiny room high up in the convent and lay down on the bed, tired but happy after her day's work.

A few items of clothing hung from the pegs on the wall, a photograph of Deborah was on the bedside table and the pink shawl lay folded neatly at the end of the bed. Otherwise the room was as it was that night in early spring when it had been her refuge.

There was a soft knock on the door, and Sister Mary Theresa came in, carrying two peaches on a plate, and a knife. 'The last two from the freezer. The new ones should by ready early next month.'

She sat on the room's only chair and expertly peeled and sliced the juicy fruit, handing pieces to Claire. 'How was Mrs McCormick today?'

'Peaceful,' Claire said. 'I have been reading *Little Women* to her. Her daughter told me it was her favourite novel and I think somewhere, down deep, she remembers the story. She doesn't speak, of course, but she has those wonderful eyes.'

'Yes, I know what you mean. I believe she will be on her way soon.'

'I see it, too.' In her time volunteering here in the hospice run by the sisters, Claire had learned to recognise the signs of a patient who was about to leave this earth. Death no longer frightened her, but instead seemed to be a natural part of the order of things.

'And what about you, Claire? When will you be on your way?'

Claire did not answer.

'Much as we have loved having you here with us, you must not use this as a hiding place from life,' the nun said softly.

'I know that. The counselling you arranged for me was valuable.' She wiped the peach juice from her hands with a paper napkin and smiled. 'I'm about ready, I think.'

'And the letter from Walker? Are you ready for that too?'

Claire thought about this for a moment. 'I just didn't want to read it until I was stronger. I don't know what is in it, but I do know it was powerful enough to help unhinge Mark.'

'You can't blame the letter or yourself for

130

that. But Mark's now getting help, and must find his own way without you.'

Claire got up and looked out of the little window, to where the sun was glinting off the water. 'I promised Deborah I would come to London for my birthday. She has an end-of-term concert and she's been working on something special to play for me.'

Claire kept looking at the sea, drawn to the ease with which the water ebbed and flowed; not resisting, just letting nature take its course.

'I will read the letter on the plane,' she said.

Twenty-Five

Claire was snug in her Virgin Atlantic upper-class suite, heading for London, and the rest of her life. Despite the food served by the airline, Claire had feasted on the picnic that Julia insisted on packing for her.

Her friends. *The posse*, as Deborah called them. She smiled just thinking about Sasha and Paulina and Julia. What would her life be without them? The letter sat on the little table in the suite, read and re-read by her and, she knew, by Mark. It must have hurt him to see those words, to feel the love, the passion that practically set fire to the pages. She did not excuse his violence. However, knowing he had seen this, helped her to understand the forces that had pushed this complex man over the edge. He had been obsessed with a fear of losing both her and Deborah.

Threats on Walker's life and hers by mobsters his father was prosecuting. Witness protection. Name changes. Years of separation, because if she had been with him, she would have been in danger.

132

It was difficult to take in all at once. But, little by little, it was beginning to make sense to her.

She remembered the guards around Walker's father that day on the court-house steps. She vaguely recalled the conviction of the so-called 'boss of bosses' at the hands of the brave Mr Kennedy. And, later, the attempt to kill him.

These long-ago events had completely changed the course of their lives. Both of their hearts had been broken. Walker didn't know he had a daughter. And Deborah didn't know about the man who gave her life.

Stop it! Claire told herself. She had promised herself before she opened the letter that she would not waste a precious moment of her new life regretting the past. She planned to hang onto what Sister Mary Theresa said when she had left the convent. 'Yesterday is not ours to recover, but tomorrow is ours to win or lose.'

She looked through the dog-eared pages to find her favourite passage.

On our day, the day we were to meet and get married, I was in the tiny village in Ireland where my mother was born. I had a new name, my mother's, and a new companion: a bodyguard who never left my side. I could only imagine how it was for you that day when I didn't come. I know what it was like for me, and I hope never to be any closer to hell than that.

But you were safe and would not have been if I had refused to go away. So I comforted myself with that.

At what would have been noon in America, I went hiking with my bodyguard, Mr O'Callaghan. I found a tiny stone chapel set into the side of a hill overlooking the River Suir and I went inside. I got down on my knees in front of the altar and I married you, Claire. I said the vows: love, honour, cherish, until death us do part. And I want you to know I have kept those vows. I have never married nor will I, because in my heart I am already married to you.

When it was safe I went back to New York looking for you. When I learned you had married and that you and your husband had a daughter, I could not bring myself to disrupt your life. I left the States for good. But I will watch you from afar and, if I ever see a chance to help you or your child, I will do it. I love her already because she is yours.

The captain announced the final approach into Heathrow. Claire wiped away a tear and carefully folded the letter into the pocket of her sweater. It felt good to have it close to her.

Once she had collected her luggage and gone through customs, the first thing Claire saw was her daughter's wild sandy curls as she leaped into the air. The hug that followed nearly toppled them both onto the floor, and there was laughter and questions and stories half told, then left aside for better ones. Yes, Deborah was still Deborah.

They were heading for the exit when Deborah pulled her aside, away from the crowd, eyes sparkling.

'Mom! I've learned the piece, the one I told you about. It was a nightmare but I did it for you. I'm playing it in my concert tomorrow.'

'*Rhapsody for Claire*. Sounds exotic.'

'It is, Mom. And sexy, I might add, just like Maestro Connelly, the composer I told you about. I don't expect to play it like he did, but maybe someday. He's an absolute genius.'

Claire hugged her daughter tightly. 'I'm sure he is.'

'He asked to come to my concert. I got him a ticket right next to you. Hope that's okay?'

'Of course it is. I'm sure we'll find plenty to talk about.'

'He's taken an interest in my playing. God knows why. Did I tell you he was the one who sent me those tickets for my birthday?'

'You didn't, but I thought it might be him.'

They went on towards the exit, arm in arm. 'Deborah dear,' Claire said casually, 'you haven't told me what the Maestro's first name is.'

'Oh, I forgot. At the Academy we have to call everyone by their proper title. It's Walker. Walker Connelly.'

'*Walker Connelly*. Yes, I rather thought that's what it would be.'

Books In The Series

Lose yourself
in a good
book with *Galaxy*®

Curled up on the sofa,
Sunday morning in pyjamas,
just before bed,
in the bath or
on the way to work?

Wherever, whenever,
you can escape
with a good book!

So go on...
indulge yourself with
a good read and the
smooth taste of
***Galaxy*® *chocolate.**

Proudly supports **Quick Reads**

Quick Reads are brilliant short new books written by bestselling writers to help people discover the joys of reading for pleasure.

Find out more at **www.quickreads.org.uk**

🐦 **@Quick_Reads**   ⓕ **Quick-Reads**

We would like to thank all our funders:

LOTTERY FUNDED

WORLD
BOOK
DAY

We would also like to thank all our partners in the Quick Reads project for their help and support: NIACE, unionlearn, National Book Tokens, The Reading Agency, National Literacy Trust, Welsh Books Council, The Big Plus Scotland, DELNI, NALA

At Quick Reads, World Book Day and World Book Night we want to encourage everyone in the UK and Ireland to read more and discover the joy of books.

World Book Day is on 6 March 2014
Find out more at **www.worldbookday.com**

World Book Night is on 23 April 2014
Find out more at **www.worldbooknight.org**

Start a new chapter

Hidden

Barbara Taylor Bradford

Drama, heartbreak and new beginnings.
This is a gripping story from a master storyteller.

On the surface, Claire Saunders has it all. She has a rewarding
career in fashion and a talented concert pianist daughter. Her
loving husband is one of the country's most trusted diplomats.

But every now and again, she has to plaster her face in heavy
make-up and wears sunglasses. She thinks she's hidden her
secret from her best friends, but they know her too well.

Can her friends get her out of harm's way and protect
her from a man who is as ruthless as he is charming and
powerful? And along the way, can Claire learn to stop
protecting the wrong people?

Harper

Start a new chapter

Blackout

Emily Barr

You wake up in a strange room,
with no idea how you got there.

You are abroad, in a city you have never visited before.

You have no money, no passport, no phone.

And there is no sign of your baby.

What do you do?

Headline Review

Start a new chapter

Rules for Dating a Romantic Hero

Harriet Evans

Do you believe in happy endings?

Laura Foster used to be a hopeless romantic. She was obsessed with meeting her own Prince Charming until she grew up and realised real life doesn't work like that.

Then she met Nick. A romantic hero straight from a fairytale, with a grand country estate and a family tree to match.

They've been together four years now and Laura can't imagine ever loving anyone the way she loves Nick.

Now, though, Nick is keeping secrets from Laura. She's starting to feel she might not be 'good enough' for his family.

Can an ordinary girl like Laura make it work with one of the most eligible men in the country?

Harper

Start a new chapter

Four Warned

Jeffrey Archer

These four short stories from a master storyteller
are packed full of twists and turns.

In Stuck on You, Jeremy steals the perfect ring for his fiancée.

Albert celebrates his 100th birthday, and is pleased
to be sent The Queen's Birthday Telegram.
Why hasn't his wife received hers?

In Russia, businessman Richard plots to murder his wife.
He thinks he's found the answer when his hotel
warns him: Don't Drink the Water.

Terrified for her life, Diana will do whatever it takes to stick to
the warning given to drivers: Never Stop on the Motorway ...

Every reader will have their favourite story – some will make
you laugh, others will bring you to tears. And every
one of them will keep you spellbound.

Pan Books

Start a new chapter

A Cruel Fate

Lindsey Davis

As long as war exists, this story will matter.

Martin Watts, a bookseller, is captured by the king's men.
Jane Afton's brother Nat is taken too. They both
suffer horrible treatment as prisoners-of-war.

In Oxford Castle jailer William Smith tortures, beats, starves
and deprives his helpless victims. Can Jane rescue her sick
brother before he dies of neglect? Will Martin dare to escape?

Based on real events in the English Civil War,
Lindsey Davis retells the grim tale of Captain Smith's
abuse of power in Oxford prison – where many
died in misery though a lucky few survived.

Hodder and Stoughton

Quick Reads

Start a new chapter

The Escape

Lynda La Plante

Is a change of identity all it takes to leave prison?

Colin Burrows is desperate. Recently sent to prison
for burglary, he knows that his four-year sentence
means he will miss the birth of his first child.

Sharing a cell with Colin is Barry Marsden. Barry likes
prison life. He has come from a difficult family and been
in and out of foster homes all his life. In prison, he has three
meals a day and has discovered a talent for drawing.
He doesn't want to leave.

Sad to see his cellmate looking depressed, Barry hatches a plan
to get Colin out of jail for the birth. It's a plan so crazy
that it might just work.

**Bestselling author Lynda La Plante's exciting tale of one
man's escape from jail is based on a true story.**

Simon & Schuster

Why not start a reading group?

If you have enjoyed this book, why not share your next Quick Read with friends, colleagues, or neighbours.

A reading group is a great way to get the most out of a book and is easy to arrange. All you need is a group of people, a place to meet and a date and time that works for everyone.

Use the first meeting to decide which book to read first and how the group will operate. Conversation doesn't have to stick rigidly to the book. Here are some suggested themes for discussions:

- How important was the plot?

- What messages are in the book?

- Discuss the characters – were they believable and could you relate to them?

- How important was the setting to the story?

- Are the themes timeless?

- Personal reactions – what did you like or not like about the book?

There is a free toolkit with lots of ideas to help you run a Quick Reads reading group at **www.quickreads.org.uk**

Share your experiences of your group on Twitter 🐦 @Quick_Reads

For more ideas, offers and groups to join visit Reading Groups for Everyone at **www.readingagency.org.uk/readinggroups**

Other resources

Enjoy this book?

Find out about all the others at **www.quickreads.org.uk**

For Quick Reads audio clips as well as videos
and ideas to help you enjoy reading visit the
BBC's Skillswise website **www.bbc.co.uk/quickreads**

Join the Reading Agency's Six Book Challenge at
www.readingagency.org.uk/sixbookchallenge

THE READING AGENCY

Find more books for new readers at
www.newisland.ie
www.barringtonstoke.co.uk

Barrington Stoke
cracking reading

Free courses to develop your skills are available in your
local area. To find out more phone 0800 100 900.

National Careers Service
Helping you take
the next step

For more information on developing your skills
in Scotland visit **www.thebigplus.com**

the big plus

Want to read more? Join your local library. You can borrow
books for free and take part in inspiring reading activities.

Want to hear more from Barbara?

barbarataylorbradford.co.uk

You can visit her website for the latest news, reviews and Barbara's own blog.

f /BarbaraTaylorBradford

Follow her on Facebook for updates on all of her books, including exclusive competitions and photos.

SECRETS FROM THE PAST

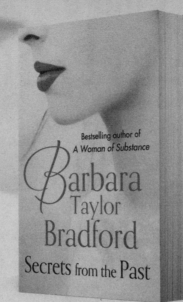

Thirty-year old Serena Stone is a talented war photographer who has followed in her famous father's footsteps. But when he dies unexpectedly, she steps away from the war zone to reassess her life. At the same time, her former lover, Zachary North, comes out of Afghanistan a broken man in desperate need of a real friend.

Serena and Zac inevitably rekindle their passion.
But when Serena stumbles across one of her father's old photographs, her whole world is turned upside down...

In search of the truth about her father, her family and her own life, Serena begins a desperate quest to uncover a story from decades earlier.

'A compulsive, emotional read about
love, lies and the ties that bind . . .'
Daily Mail

CAVENDON HALL

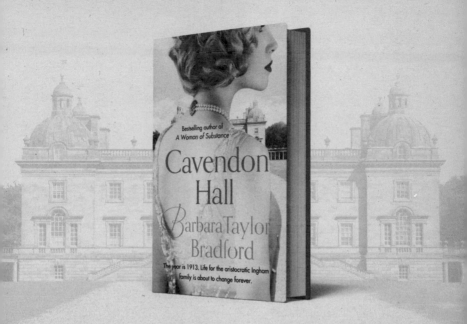

Two entwined families: the aristocratic Inghams and the Swanns who serve them. The Earl and Countess have relied on their faithful retainers Alice and Walter Swann as their young family grows up.

One stately home: Cavendon Hall, a grand imposing house nestled in the beautiful Yorkshire Dales

A society beauty: Lady Daphne Ingham is the most beautiful of the Earl's four daughters. Being presented at Court and making a glittering marriage is her destiny.

But in the summer of 1913, a devastating event changes her future forever, and threatens the Ingham name. Yet life as the families of Cavendon Hall know it - Royal Ascot, supper dances, grouse season feasts and a full servants' hall - is about to alter beyond recognition as the storm clouds of war gather.